Praise for

The Village Maestro

"...exceptional. Can't put *Maestro* down."
—**Dr. Richard Newkirk,
Brain Expert, USA**

"From the moment you read the first sentence of each story, you find yourself immersed in a different world. Each parable contains a universe in its core with pithy learning embedded in its fabric. In a world that is constantly searching for meaning, these stories provide one with a sense of spiritual relief and intuitive wisdom; an intangible feeling that stays with you long after the story is finished."
—**Soven Trehan,
American Express, Delhi**

"Brimming with astute narratives, the reader is afforded brief, brilliant tales that speak to the soul. Wise vignettes from history and literature give insight into life lessons for today's modern world."
—**Sarah Bergstedt,
Minneapolis, USA**

"I am continually perplexed and impressed; the cadence in which Dr. Mathai tells these stories carries that same casual, consecrated genius that made his classes at Judson uniquely special to me. I was, more than once, teary-eyed reading them."
—**Erik Berger,
Artist, Fukuoka, Japan**

"Through his quick, masterful tales, Varghese Mathai engages us in pondering an array of life lessons. But don't get fooled by the brevity of the encounter-- the stories may be very short, yet you'll find yourself reflecting on them for years to come. Great teachers have a way of starting a story that our minds don't want to end--even when we've finished the course or closed the book!"

—Dr. Joyce Weinsheimer,
Georgia Institute of Technology

"A narrative told artfully is powerful, and Dr. Mathai's concise and gifted storytelling style brought these tales to life...I'm happy to see that this collection of insightful stories will finally be reaching a larger audience. I believe they will be read and reread, time and time again."

—Patrick Endres,
Wildlife Photographer, Alaska, USA

"I recall the popular treat of a parable with an unfailing punchline marking the start of each of Professor Mathai's lectures. The mastery of the art of the telling lay in its brilliant brevity, charged with spiritual insight. Now that The Village Maestro is poised to sojourn across the world, it's going to create a family of very, very happy readers"

—Mark Trescott,
Walworth Barbour International School, Israel

The Village MAESTRO

&

100 Other Stories

The Village Maestro, 2021. Erik Berger. Acrylic & Gouache.

The Village
MAESTRO
&
100 Other Stories

VARGHESE MATHAI

Privately published for the author by

An imprint of
Salt Desert Media Group Limited,
7 Mulgrave Chambers, 26 Mulgrave Rd,
Sutton SM2 6LE, England, UK.
Email: publisher@pipparannbooks.com
Website: www.pipparannbooks.com

ISBN 978-1-913738-82-2

Designed, illustrated, and typeset by Erik Berger

PRINTED IN THE UNITED STATES OF AMERICA

Dedicated to

Rani V. Mathai

A great but unsung hero
to whose sacrificial love and unseen service for others
I am the only human witness

Contents

Foreword

The world lives by storytelling and has now become even more lively with the publication of *The Village Maestro & 100 Other Stories* by Dr. Varghese Mathai, Professor of English at Judson University in Elgin, Illinois, USA. This book is a collection of over 100 fables, parables, and picks from folklore that Dr. Mathai has used as openers in his classes over the past thirty years. It is a treasure trove of moral stories, virtuous lessons, sermonic support material and inspirational reading for a multicultural audience.

A native of Kerala, India, Dr. Mathai completed his PhD at Baylor University in Texas and thus has a wonderful grasp of both sides of the globe. East meets west on Dr. Mathai's desk. He is a Fulbright Scholar and yet enjoys teaching freshman level literature and composition courses. He writes with authority using short parables from the Jewish tradition, Chaucer, India, San Francisco, South Africa, New Orleans, England, France, Egypt and even from the former-planet, Pluto. *The Village Maestro* is both a joyous romp and thought-provoking read.

Dr. Mathai was one of the most relational professors with whom I have worked. Our first conversation was about St. Thomas and the Thomist Church of South India. He is comfortable and unthreatened while discussing higher education, Christianity, domestic life, Hinduism and even world politics. Students benefited from his classes because he accepted nothing less than the best from himself and his scholars.

The unique character of his classes was the subject of many late-night dormitory conversations about Dr. Mathai. He began each class with a parable and students would attend class just to hear this thought for the day. One day might be about the healing power of cobra venom followed the next day with a morality lesson based on Haitian refugees. The next week students would get a thought from the Mosaic Tabernacle, the Golden Gate Bridge or compass legs in a John Donne poem.

Sometimes the vignettes seem like they came from Jesus, Will Rogers or the Brothers Grimm while others came from the challenges of daily living. Because of his background and education in India, *The Village Maestro* has an Eastern glow which adds mystery and power to each parable. Each microstory comes alive when read aloud as if told by the ancient village shaman or as a modern TED Talk.

The Village Maestro & 100 Other Stories is a way to learn about the world at a distance or about myself up close, as we engage the wisdom of the ages through the stories of today. "Once upon a time" now becomes contemporary time.

Jerry B. Cain, Chancellor
Judson University
Elgin, Illinois, USA

Acknowledgments

I express my deep gratitude to my beloved friends who have cordially supported the publication of this book. Much help was necessary along the way for everything from the preparation of the manuscript to the logistics of production and delivery.

Poet and publisher Professor Prabhu Guptara of Pippa Rann Books & Media has been the most recent of the manuscript's talented readers. His feedback took the entire text through a tough regimen of body checks. As a publisher, he didn't tire of tracking the step by step progress of this book over a very long time. Without his perceptive questions and brisk arguments in the margins I could have been much less on my guard against slips in several places. I thank him for the time and skills that he has so kindly invested in producing this book.

The manuscript had been ready for a while, even before it had landed on Prof Guptara's desk. Anissa Stringer, published author and senior editor at Ruffalo Noel Levitz, read the text two years earlier and gave me comments from a reader perspective. A few months thereafter, Dr. Jerry Cain,

Judson University's chancellor, read the full digital draft and recommended it for consideration by an established American publisher. Their response was positive, but another direction eventually became necessary. Dr. Cain's recommendation of the book gave a fillip to the spirits of the author who now has the added joy of thanking him for his voice in the book through his charming preface for it.

Because I have been in academic migrant labor, my career history shows a kind of global weave. Nonetheless, a lot of good people in the scattered places of I've served have either heard my stories or about them, and have now provided support for these stories to reach their alumni who were my students. Among them are Mary Dulabaum, Communications Director of Judson University, my home institution; Kristen Eagen, Vice President of Judson's Alumni Relations; and Stephanie Kleczynski, Assistant Director of Alumni Relations, also of Judson. Erik Berger, an alumnus of Judson and my former student, designed a splendid cover for the book and gave the Maestro a touching endorsement. Over in Minnesota, likewise, I am blessed with the welcoming voices of Dr. Gary Benedict, former president of Crown College, and Julie Howe, Director of Crown's External Relations. Award-winning wildlife photographer Patrick Endres, a former student at Crown, has lovingly provided moral support for the effort of bringing this book to birth, as well as kept a book order ready for a first edition copy for a very long time.

And how could I ever thank all my students in front of whom I appeared with my daily piece as an avatar of the Village Maestro? Their addiction to hearing my story each day, and their insistence on catching any story that they missed, and then requesting a collection of the stories in the form of this book, all came together to result in this collection. In turn, through these parabolic tales, a lot of tender human connections have become possible with a whole generation of students.

All of my students and the good people mentioned here are God's gift to me; they certainly appear in the listing of my life's capital assets. My debt to all of them is immense. I thank all of them for the space they have allowed me in their lives.

Introduction

The Story of the Maestro Stories

Still young and fresh out of an American graduate school, I started teaching at LeTourneau University in Texas. My department chair had some preparatory instructions for me, all of which seemed familiar. However, at the end of our brief chat he said, "Oh, for class devotions, you can circulate a sign-up sheet. Call the students forward each day, by turn."

"Sure," I said. We shook hands and parted. I had no idea what "class devotions" were, but nervous vanity prevented me from asking.

The next day I was in my first class, still no better informed about class devotions than I was the day before. After the initial exchange of courtesies, I passed around a sign-up sheet. With no sign of surprise whatsoever, around ten students put their names down. The rest of the class didn't.

On Day Two, the first volunteer came forward. The eyes of all were on him at the lectern. He mumbled something for about a minute, cocked his cap, and went back to his seat. "That was devotions?" I asked in my naïve plainness.

"Yap," he said.

"That was reassuring," I said to myself.

Day Three, I called up the next fellow on the list. He gave a recital of similar length and content as did his peer the day before. The audience seemed to have been expecting nothing more from the ritual, and the speaker knew it. I still wasn't sure what was happening.

Then came the fourth day. The Man of the Day begged to be excused because he was "not prepared." I called the next student, thinking that he might perhaps step in. But he wasn't "prepared" either.

I then said to the class: "Okay, let's do this: I think I get the idea. You are asked to bring a thought or a reflection as a tone setter for the start of the class each day, right?"

"Yes," they said.

"If so," I added, "Why don't *I do this* whenever we meet, unless of course, you wish to?" The relief the class felt was hugely visible. This was too good an offer to pass up. Even the sullen scholar in the back corner was nodding, pleased.

From the next class onwards, I started telling them something each day, anecdotally. Shortly I realized that each day's narrative (unscripted) took the shape of a parable or a microstory. The matter came from an array of sources—history, literature, philosophy, science, religion, media events, and what not. Eventually there was an assumption that my class would by default start with a story of the day, and it worked out to be that way. Students who missed a class would often come to my office the next day asking for the story missed. For a long time, privately I called it "the class opener."

Well, the story stuck. I moved on from Texas to other places like the University of St. Thomas in Minnesota, the University of Minnesota, and to Judson University in Illinois. Between my first story at LeTourneau University and the latest at Judson, a whole generation has passed. Alumni have called me at times to refresh a story for their own use. Many have asked for the stories in the form of a volume. That's when I thought that perhaps I should do a "century" of them as a trial run.

The story is the maker of legacies. A culture lives the story it has been told. The differences in strength between one nation and another may well be in the core story that it has believed and lived out. The difference between winning and losing was often in the appealing story.

In all traditions of learning, Eastern or Western, Semitic or Asian, exercises of logic, law, language, or the sciences, came in the form of stories. Classical sages hardly ever taught except through riddles, fables, and parables

The Indian novelist who was also a Nobel nominee, R. K. Narayan, has a rural hero called Nambi for one of his short stories. Every night Nambi drew an eager village crowd under a banyan tree to hear one of his stories, which habitually mesmerized the village folk. The stories kept coming night after night, for years, as if from some perpetual store. One night, nonetheless, for the first time in his life, Nambi felt his words trail and the story stall. Repeat attempts to resume only made his slip heavier. This was a telltale sign of his career as a storyteller ending. He lived for a while longer yet, but having nothing more to say. Our meaning is in our story.

All tales must end, and so must the time granted to their tellers. The classroom has been my village. There, young people with loving hearts bade me bring out as a book what I had shared in this mode. I am pleased to oblige.

Varghese Mathai
Chicago, IL
September 2021

The Stories

Story #1
The Teacher's Pet

Desert Father Sylvannus of Egypt had twelve disciples living as a community of monks under him. These men owned nothing. Devotional life and charitable services to the needy essentially filled their time. Extreme austerity, personal purity, and absolute submission to authority were the norms of desert holiness. Closeness to the life of Christ was the ardent goal of their life.

Abba Sylvannus had a favorite among the twelve, at least so believed the other eleven, and they felt a little jealous about it. Rather than bring the matter to their master openly, they sought the help of an elderly monk from another community to mediate the issue with Sylvannus. The visitor arrived as appointed, greeted Sylvannus, and quickly came to the charge of favoritism. Instead of giving an immediate answer in defense, Sylvannus calmly took the visitor for a quick tour of his desert cells.

They came to the first cell door, and Sylvannus knocked. "Brother," he called.

"Yes, Abba," came the polite answer from within.

"I need you for a moment; would you mind?" Sylvannus asked.

"No at all, Abba, give me just one minute," came the reply. A minute passed, but the door still stayed shut. They moved on to the second door, and again Sylvannus knocked and called, "Brother," and there was a quick answer from inside.

"I need you for a little help!" said the monk, as before.

"Certainly, Abba, I'll be out right away," promised the disciple inside, but the door stood shut.

On to the third door they went, knocking again and repeating his call. He did not see the third brother, nor the fourth, nor the fifth, nor the tenth, nor even the eleventh.

Now they were at the twelfth door.

"Brother Mark," called Sylvannus.

"Yes, Abba," came the answer from a young man who appeared instantly at the open door. He had a stylus in one hand.

"What were you doing, brother?" asked Sylvannus.

"Copying," he answered. "May I take a look, please?" asked the elderly hermit. Greatly pleased, Mark led the elder and his guest to a parchment which still had the ink wet on the half-finished letter "Omega."

Sylvannus gave his guest a pointed look.

Story #2
The Masterly Slave

We all know Cicero, the great Roman history maker. Julius Caesar sought his friendship and public support but got neither. The man was a lawyer, philosopher, writer, orator and senator of Rome. For over a thousand years, Europe considered him the gold standard for writing and public speaking.

Of all of Cicero's treasures, one was priceless: a slave born in his own household, named Tiro. In his *De Republica*, Cicero says that conquered people might rightly remain as slaves if they were unable to govern themselves. Yet, as life goes, Tiro the slave was to govern Cicero's affairs as his confidant, secretary, manager, editor, biographer, and the very preserver of Cicero's legacy. Tiro's absence would distress Cicero and even his family. Slaves of his day were often employed as pedagogues, physicians, musicians, artisans, armorers, weavers, jewelers and what not. Not surprisingly then, Tiro had multiple roles.

Tiro is known in history as the father of stenography, which he invented to record the orations of Cicero. An author in his own right, Tiro also wrote the biography of Cicero, besides editing, arranging and even publishing his master's works. Tiro survived Cicero by nearly four decades as a free man, securing the fame of his slain master.

Nothing matches the beauty of merit reigning from its rightful seat.

Story #3
LeMaster's Dedication

D r. Jim LeMaster was an excellent teacher and industrious scholar. One day I took the liberty of leafing through a volume of poems that I noticed on his desk. The work was dedicated to a certain university man. I asked LeMaster who this man was whom he chose to honor in this way. He told me that it was a professor of his own, to whom he had submitted a set of poems in his early student days. The professor gave his feedback in unveiled ridicule before the entire class. The public insult only strengthened LeMaster's resolve to improve on his craft aggressively. I asked him if he sent a copy of the book to the insensitive professor. He said that he did.

I should have asked LeMaster if he had taken the idea for such a brilliant reprisal from E. E. Cummings whose novel *The Enormous Room* was dedicated to the fifteen publishers who had rejected it, one after the other. Cummings ultimately published it on his own, and it has since become a major title.

Many publishing houses have researched their own archives to learn to their embarrassment how many heavyweights they had cast away from their estate—H. G. Wells, George Orwell, and Herman Melville being a short example set. *The San Francisco Examiner* told Nobel Laureate Rudyard Kipling that he didn't know how to use the English language!

Time has a way of showing builders that the stone that they had rejected was perhaps the cornerstone.

Story #4
The Czar Child

P eter the Great of Russia had to grow up at high stress speed to seize his place. His father, Czar Alexis, died when Peter was nine. At the age of ten, Peter and his mentally-challenged brother stood as joint Czars of Russia, with their twenty-five year-old half-sister Sophia acting as regent. Sophia was the thirteenth daughter in the first marriage of Peter's father, and she wanted to stand in Peter's place. The rifts and intrigues between the claimants to the throne were deep and befuddling, as illustrated by Peter and the scheming Sophia.

Czar Alexis had secured a brilliant teacher for Peter, in the person of General Paul Menesius, a learned Scot skilled in military tactics. Menesius lived in the palace itself, training the prince who loved his teacher. Sophia, however, wanted the General to release Peter from his care. Knowing Sophia's intent, General Menesius refused, and Sophia dismissed him.

Before bidding farewell, the General charged Peter, barely a teenager then, to resist every temptation, to flee idleness, and to acquire all useful knowledge with extreme diligence.

Sophia sent Peter to a palace in a small village outside Moscow. She arranged fifty playmates to amuse him and to live with him in unrestrained indulgence. The design was to ruin Peter by wild living.

His teacher's counsel, given with foresight, had already taken a hold of Peter. He knew that what appeared as "play" was not play at all, but a deadly snare. Peter turned every "amusement" into a useful art. In music he learned the use of drums and practiced it to fit the military beat and signals. Hands-on crafts took the mode of military engineering and artillery. He made tools and implements with his own hands. Every "playmate" became a battle peer. By the time he was to leave the "playing fields," he had already created a full-fledged military school on the site. Many believe it was the moral foundation put in place by his teacher that led Peter to greatness.

I wonder if the General had not, consciously or otherwise, applied to Peter the words that had, long ago been written by Paul in his famous letter to Timothy: Flee youthful lusts; let no man slight your youth.

Story #5
Claims of Leverage

Archimedes famously said, "Give me a place to stand, and I will move the earth."

A lever gives enormous mechanical advantage in moving weights with minimal physical exertion to the operator. Tilt a see-saw, split a log, lift a sunken ship or a whole bridge, knock down a massive boulder atop a hill, or raise a finished tower to its place: it is all the work of the lever. Primitive humans and their modern counterparts match the use of the lever in their own turns.

I heard someone say that a certain amount of money as pension funds had given great "leverage" to a city. People talk about the political "leverage" of power brokers with the right connections to public figures. We already know of the dream leverage of star power in political campaigns, corporate boards, and activist bodies.

It is fascinating to see that the human frame as a system of levers making possible its stability, flexibility, and movement. We use our own levers in the body to rock a baby on our knees or to pick off the speck of dust from our eye.

But it gets better. There are motions of our heart that target results and succeed. Even better, the human soul is equipped with enormous "leverage" to connect to the seat of cosmic power. A person in unnoticed privacy connects to the Almighty, and each time it happens, the world itself moves toward God. There you have both the lever in hand and a place to stand.

Story #6
The Trees of Belize

Belize was a very poor Central American country in the early twentieth century. Not very large in size or population still, its main source of income is tourism.

A woman from the US once made her home here in one of its quiet villages. She ran a small restaurant to support herself, but her goal of wanting to live in Belize was to save its seemingly endangered iguanas, reptiles that look like large lizards. She turned her wooded backyard into an iguana habitat.

A large tree with a sign stood right behind her restaurant. On its massive trunk hung a shingle with the phrase POISON TREE lettered on it. Just touching the bark of the tree would cause the skin to itch and to flare up. Contact with the leaves would make it worse.

Within fifty yards of the Poison Tree stood another tree, bearing another sign: MEDICINE TREE. In age and size both looked comparable. Why was it called "the medicine tree"? Well, if anyone touched the poison tree and felt any irritation by it, a little rub with a few leaves of the medicine tree would undo the effects of the poison!

Yes, the threat of evil is universal, but lest it take the world over, some healing tree stands within reach. There is no malady in this cosmos without a remedy to undo its power, says the tree.

Story #7
A Soldier's Stride

I had the pleasure of living in an official military zone for a year. One could feel the secure air of authority in this solid world of discipline where tens of thousands of troops lived. Their day started with the morning drill at 5:30. Early in the afternoon they were home, except those serving in later shifts.

One evening I noticed a mid-level officer of the morning units putting on his action gear. I asked him what he was preparing for.

"Night rounds," he said.

"Where?" I asked.

"In the market square," he said, with an on-duty face.

I looked at him rather puzzled, thinking he was being sarcastic, but he appeared every bit serious, like a sentry at a fortress. He added that he would be working for the next six hours in the town market.

"To do what, if I may ask?" I queried.

"To patrol the bazaar for any wandering soldiers," he replied.

Apparently, there were places in the market district where a soldier should not be found.

"But they wouldn't wear the uniform in off-duty hours, especially if they could be caught, so how will you catch them?" I went on.

"Mister, a soldier can spot another soldier from a mile away, in a mere glance," he stated, with the ring of a proverb.

"How?" I was all the more curious.

"Why, just by the way he walks!" he said, with no bravado in his tone.

That showed me how sharp my learning curve was. The manner of a person's steps or stride gives him away. In the military, they first make a man unlearn the way he is used to walking, and then train him the way he should, until the stride of it becomes his new nature. When those trained steps go astray, the watchful eye spots them.

Story #8
Fenelon as Teacher

"The Little Terror"—that was the childhood fame of the Duke of Burgundy, the grandson of Louis XIV of France. Heir to the throne, the little duke was a royal pain. The renowned Bishop Fenelon was the king's choice for his grandson's tutor. So popular was Fenelon as a human being that when his own nation was involved in the continental war of Spanish Succession, the forces on both sides arranged for his protection.

The little kid was a school unto himself, and Fenelon was the only mortal on earth able to run that school. He told the palace staff to simply ignore his pupil's frequent fits of rage. Now he needed a curriculum. Homer was a common text for European schools. Fenelon chose the Iliad story of Ulysses' son, and wrote a novel of sorts entitled *Télémaque* for his pupil. The work had a hidden goal of showing contexts of kingly behavior through the adventures of Telemachus. Of course, when the prelate equated the self-willed duke with the Greek prince, the appeal to his adolescent pride was of epic measure. The bishop's strong moral firmness, blended with his love, did the rest of the lad's taming, and the young Duke of Burgundy developed deep affection for Fenelon.

There is a Fenelon for every Louis. Bringing the two together is the making of history.

Story #9
Scudder on Agazziz

Louis Agazziz was a renowned professor and the founder of Harvard Museum of Comparative Zoology. Samuel Scudder, a younger naturalist, joined him as a short-term research associate. At their first meeting, Agazziz took Scudder to the lab, pulled out a fish from its alcohol jar, and laid it in a tray.

"Take this fish and look at it. We call it a haemulon. By and by I will ask you what you have seen," said Agazziz, and then he left the place. The "look" was to be just that—observation with plain eyes, without the use of any lab instruments.

Scudder looked over the preserved fish, and within moments decided that he had seen all there was to see of it. Then he wandered over to the more attractive locations of the museum. Several hours later Agazziz returned, and Scudder stood ready. He described the fish in reasonable detail, but the professor told the young man that he had missed the most conspicuous parts. Scudder returned to the lab for an afternoon for yet a closer look, which helped little. The professor advised him to put the fish aside and to review it mentally, overnight.

"The fish had symmetrical sides and organs," Scudder reported in the morning, which impressed Agazziz, but there had to be more. Attempts continued, each winning some approval from Agazziz, with more still left to cover. Scudder handled the fish for a few more days with occasional discoveries to report.

"Look, look, look!" the professor kept urging him. Once Scudder was done with the fish, a second one was assigned for comparison, and then a third, and so on.

Months later, Scudder and friends chalked up, just for amusement, the shapes of grotesque looking creatures on the Museum blackboard. Among them were a few fish sketches. Agazziz noticed them. "Every one of them is a haemulon!" commented the professor, and he knew who had drawn them. As for Scudder himself, each time he drew a fish from then on, it would turn out to be a haemulon!

Scudder left Harvard on his way to greatness, thankful for the legacy from Agazziz, the acquired habit of learning by thorough observation. It was "of inestimable value," Scudder said, which he could not earn any other way, nor part with. Seeing, we sometimes see not, disabled only by our abilities!

Story #10
Stately Perks

Feeling free enough with the folksy manner of President George W. Bush, an Argentine reporter turned to some personal questions. "What do you have on you when you go about, Mr. President?" asked the man.

"Es Todo," said Bush, meaning, "this is it," showing his handkerchief and the inexpensive Timex with the monogrammed "W" on the dial. Bush added that the President had little use of a wallet, cell phone or car keys, because his aides would attend to the needs of all such.

I recall reading about the official travel accounts of several US presidents. One report noted that more than seventy planes made up the presidential fleet of Bill Clinton on his India visit. The President's staff, advisors, experts, invited business groups, hundreds of journalists, security corps, and many more could be in it. They go by default, because the President is traveling. No one is surprised that he would have a large entourage. When the President travels, the power of his state moves with him.

Christ told a large audience on a mountain: "Seek ye first the kingdom of God, and all these things will be added unto you." For most of us, the labor of life is mostly to acquire "these things." What if, instead, "these things" were pursuing us, since we are set on things far better? Jesus himself sent forth his disciples on their mission and asked them not to take their wallet, staff, and extras as travelers do, yet they were hosted by the elite of the cities they visited.

Story #11
The Fig Tree

I recall a casual meeting with a fellow student out on a walk during my earlier college days. He told me that he was from the distant countryside, the only son of disabled parents confined to their home. He would therefore go home every other week or so to make sure that they had all the supplies needed, including drinking water. I was very impressed with the account of his filial care. He quickly added that he was also a lay preacher. At this, my esteem for him rose even higher. Soon we had a schedule of regular walks together, and good discussions along the way. Often, he would comment upon the Bible of which I knew very little, and about the little I knew, I had unending questions.

One of those evenings he quizzed me: "Do you know this story of Jesus cursing a fig tree because he found no fruit in it?"

My ears perked up. I had read that portion in Mark 11 and in Matthew 21. It had bothered me that Jesus would be upset with a barren tree.

"Do you know what that means?" he asked, sensing that I didn't.

"No," I said, hoping that he might say more about it. He seemed, however, to show no eagerness to enlighten me any further, though he appeared confident of the meaning.

"Would you mind telling me what that could be?" I asked, rather imploringly.

His face showed a steely look. "Nope!" came his slapping reply, and then he turned around and walked away.

"Goodness, what a jerk!" I said to myself in disbelief.

I have never seen him since.

I could think of none on my campus that could interpret this curious gospel story. About six months later—and I had been thinking about this withered tree all along—I had a surprise call from the Lions governor, a wealthy plantation man, inviting me as a student speaker at their state conference.

A few weeks later I arrived at his mansion, as appointed. I had to wait a little for my turn, so his steward offered to give me a tour of the estate garden, all filled with exotic plants and fruit trees. I noticed a midsize tree, lush in its cascading leaves, each the size of an ancient war shield, gleaming in lively green. It seemed to sit on the ground, shaped overall like a large Moghul dome.

I asked the steward what tree this was. "The fig tree," he said.

"The fig tree?" I echoed back in surprise.

"Yes," came his low-key reply.

"The fig tree, did you say?" I asked again.

"Yes," the man assured me, obviously wondering about my excitement. I asked to be excused; he moved on. I walked around that tree a few times like a tickled squirrel, and then paused; then I parted its cloaking foliage, which to my sheer marvel, gave way and led me to the clear view of its trunk. And what did I see within? Scores of ripe fruit, the size of tennis balls on long stems from the trunk and the branches. I plucked one of them, bit into it and got nothing but a watery taste. I threw the fruit away.

In an instant, I recognized something: this tree would look the same, with or without fruit, to a passerby. If it had fruit, it would make no boastful show of it, which might be a good quality; but if it held no fruit, then too, the rich leaves would cover its barrenness, thus fooling one into thinking that it might have great yield inside. That very instant I thought that Jesus could have been giving a figurative lesson on the nation of Israel: The fig tree was Israel; he was its great gardener, looking for fruit and finding no fruit in the tree of his own planting. A fruitless tree signals its own doom by the axe and fire. Prophet Micah gives the idyllic picture of the elderly sitting under the fig tree, watching their little ones play. Consider such a national symbol being so barren, yet hiding that curse with its gleaming cover.

I did not have to go to Israel for the rest of the story. It is my own hypocrisy that I tend to hide with the beguiling blanket of green.

Story #12
From Beggar to Bride

L
ord Tennyson's short poem, "The Beggar Maid," tells the story of the surprise appearance of a beggar maid in an African monarch's court. The King's men, seated in ranks, are engaged in the business of the occasion. Then, a stunning beauty, wrapped in little more than tattered rags, paces into the scene. The court freezes, and time stands still. She speaks not a word: one look, that's all it took for His Majesty to step down from his throne to greet and to lead the stray guest to the midst of the court. The lords are rhapsodic in their praise for the maid: each notes some mark or measure of her beauty or the grace of her move. One praises her ankle, one her eyes, and another her lovely mien. Rare as such an event is in a palace hall, so is her beauty. Her image is loveliness sculpted. King Cophetua decrees in the hearing of all, "This beggar maid shall be my queen."

You may say that this is what happens when God sees the human soul. God sees His own image in anyone, even in the supposed slave or a beggar. In our clouded notions about God, we only wander now and then toward His Mercy Seat, expecting a little dole for the day, ignorant of the self-giving benevolence of the King. Spiritually, we live far beneath our means, and needlessly so. The daring move of the first step into the King's Hall is an intelligent, redemptive act. In our baring of the self, the Maker of it falls in instant love with it. The shape that has borne the soul as a beggar finds itself turned into the Bride.

Story #13
A Citizen at Sea

A live news story showed a crowded rowboat of Haitian refugees approaching the Florida coast. The plain and old wooden boat was not meant for a sea trip of any kind at all. Utterly devoid of any safety rig, it had merely an open huddle space for about ten, but over thirty desperate men and women were on board, clutching on to the edges. The storms were too strong even well-built vessels, so what might befall this one was anyone's guess. Its huddlers got thrown from one end to the other, and eventually one end of the boat stood pitched upward, sliding all of them down to the sinking end and from there slung over to the swelling tides. The US Coast Guard, on patrol, sped toward them. Their skill and speed helped rescue nearly all of them. Since the Haitians had entered the US territorial waters without permit, the rescue also meant their arrest, but the law would be kinder than the devouring depths.

Among the number brought on board was a fully pregnant woman. She went into labor within minutes, right under the flag mast. Whether out of stress or having come to the fullness of time, she gave birth to a baby boy in a providential delivery. Almost like Moses, this child, was drawn out of the waters which could well have been his grave, as well as his mother's, but the woman received the immediate tidings that her son, born on a US vessel, was thereby legally a US citizen that very minute! As if to declare it to the wider world, the mother and son had the stars and stripes capering over them. I suppose the State didn't have to look far for a ready wet nurse.

Story #14
An Unplanned Flight

S ome time ago, I had to book an emergency flight to Mumbai, to see my father at a hospital in that city. The travel agent asked me if I had a route preference. The Middle East was generally difficult then, so I told him to get me an alternative, if possible. He agreed.

On the JFK runway the captain announced that we were on our eleven-hour non-stop ride to Cairo—the first leg of my flight—not the route I had been promised. I flared up within at the evident slip of my agent, but there was little I could do about it. We landed in Cairo the next day at 2:00 PM local time. The onward passengers were to stay seated in the plane for the two-hour transit break while the aircraft had its clean up and crew change. In the roasting heat of the desert, they had the doors of the plane open for the entire time, while the moaning machines rolled through the aisles.

The journey resumed as per schedule. Annoying announcements came by the minute. As soon as the climb leveled off, a stewardess warned: "Ladies and gentlemen, please be advised that photographing the topography is not permitted."

"Are you kidding?" I said to myself; "How many shots of these sand dunes could one want?"

Five minutes later it was the pilot's turn: "Ladies and gentlemen, over to your right is the Red Sea." I nosed my way to the window, but alas, there was no sea to see. As if to have me not lose heart, he piped up again, "Now, to your left is Mount Sinai." I was excited. I had heard and read quite a bit about this great mountain. Now it was right underneath me. I looked, and, indeed, there it was, for a good few moments. The sight was utterly underwhelming. That famed mountain stood on its vastly barren terrain, with scarcely a green shoot anywhere. It just sat there like a massive lump of molten copper, radiating killer heat, for all I could tell. Then I thought of its many stately rivals, any of which could easily eclipse it. Sinai was hostile, barren, rocky, even ugly. I felt cheated by the impressions I had gained of it from my readings in the past. Still fuming inside at my travel agent, I kept ranting and raving inwardly. Then, from within rose a soundless statement: "Yes, but in spite of it all, this is the mountain the Lord chose for His meeting with His people!"

A humbling peace settled into my heart. All my pent up rage dissolved. The rest of my trip to Mumbai, with one or two more imposed stops still en route, seemed no burden at all. If God were to choose a place on the basis of its aesthetics or territorial glory for Moses' encounter with him, there indeed were plenty of other sites. But the most unlikely is often His normal choice. While the majestic ranges of the Alps or Bashaan command awe in their viewers, they matter little in the light of what Sinai saw and heard. It took me an unsought tour through the desert to learn that lesson.

Story #15
The Village Maestro

A handful of my heroes have no idea how much I adore them. I doubt that any of them would even recognize me. Some I may have met casually, just once or so; others have lived and passed on well before my time, even centuries ago.

The remarkable man I recall for this moment was a retired music teacher, four foot five or so, of an Indian village. Dark skinned and toothless, he went about with a harmonium, singing old hymns wherever the opportunity occurred. He neither sought nor received an invitation to perform; after all, how many bookings could you expect for a sixty-five-year-old, sans teeth?

I saw him at a small cottage gathering where he showed up unexpectedly. People were respectful of him, calling him "Aasaan," meaning "Maestro." He spoke with no persuasive charm, nor made any effort to create new friendships. He sang a little hymn and played his instrument. He never expected, nor took, a gift from anyone.

The Maestro owned a small house on a half-acre rural lot. Land was pricy where he lived. People made sure that their property boundaries were inviolable, but not this man. One of his neighbors was in the habit of readjusting the fence for slight outward expansion every spring. The old man knew it, but never bothered. One particular year, this neighbor moved the fence a good three feet into the Maestro's property. It was a move outrageous enough for all of the neighbors to notice. They waited for the man's return from his regular itinerant trip.

Back home within a week, the man set down his instrument on the porch wall and gave himself a little stretch in his canvas recliner. The neighbors seemed far too eager to deliver the news to him. "Maestro," said one, "The man next door has moved the fence three feet into your property, the whole stretch." The old man said nothing. They were expecting a showdown between him and the encroacher. They tried the juicy line again. "Aasaan, didn't you hear what we said? The guy next door has seized more of your land, sir."

Ever so calmly, the Maestro answered. "My friends, you have been so kind as to bring me this news. Do me yet another favor, if you will. Tell him to help himself to the rest of what I have, too. If you think I would fight over this clod, you must be all wet."

Here, I thought, was a prince of heaven, one whom even an outright land grab could not provoke. An emperor could not despoil him, for his wealth was indexed far too high.

Story #16
Two Brothers

Jewish lore speaks of two brothers who lived on their inherited family farm. Settled on either side of a hill, they worked hard and enjoyed plenteous harvests. One of them was married and had a happy family, while the other remained single. The brothers loved each other deeply.

At one of the harvests the single brother said to himself, "The Lord gave me good crops as He always does. I have plenty to live on and have little care. See my brother, though. He has the burden of a family. I must do something to cheer him up a little." That night, he hauled a large measure of his grain in several trips to his brother's threshing floor, added it to his pile and slipped away unnoticed each time.

The next day, the other brother, who had also been thinking about his single sibling, said to himself, "The Lord has given me a good harvest even this year as He always does. I have a lovely wife and godly children. We are all healthy and happy. As for my brother, he has known nothing but the pain of lonely labor. I must do something to give him a good moment." That night, he too hauled several loads of his grain to secretly add to his brother's grain heap, and came away unnoticed.

The brothers eventually made a habit of this secret hauling of their harvest grain during every season. Each chose the time and manner best suited for his secret task. One night, the older brother was climbing the hill slope, sweating and heaving under the weight of his grain sack. From the other side he heard the heavy breath and steps of someone thudding toward him. They bumped into each other at the summit, and each knew who the other was, right away. They dropped their loads and fell on each other's neck, weeping. Jewish tradition says that the spot where the brothers met is the site that Solomon chose to build the Temple of God.

Story #17
The Man Who
Feared the Song

In his famous history of the English people, the Venerable Bede devoted a portion for a poor cowherd called Caedmon who kept the stables of the Abbey of Whitby. It was customary for residents of this monastic house to entertain themselves on occasion by singing in turns while playing on the harp. Caedmon dreaded the moment because he had neither learning nor singing skill. When he saw the harp start at one end, he would excuse himself for some pretend errand outside. One night he used the usual ruse to slip away to the stable. There he lay and fell asleep. Soon he had a dream in which a man bade him, of all things, to sing a song. He protested that he could not. The man insisted that he must.

"Of what?" Caedmon asked.

"Sing of the beginning of created beings," said the man. That very moment Caedmon began singing songs he had never known, in words he had never learned.

The next morning, with all of the dream-songs fast in his memory, the cowherd told the town-reeve what happened to him. The reeve took him to Abbess Hilda of Whitby. The Abbess assembled the learned men and scholars to hear Caedmon recite his songs. Having heard him, the scholars gave him "other stories and words of knowledge," urging him to deliver them too in verse.

"Able to learn all that he heard, and keeping it all in mind," says Bede, "like a clean animal chewing the cud, [he] turned it into the sweet song."

Caedmon's teachers themselves "wrote and learned at his mouth," his songs on stories on the holy writ and teachings of diverse kinds.

A man without a song becomes known only for his song.

Story #18
The Cannibal Call

A rmin Meiwes is a name I cite, only to show what sanity defies as possible: he was a German computer engineer who ran an internet ad for a good-looking male of healthy build, of about thirty years of age, whom he wanted to slaughter and eat. Several young Germans responded, but eventually begged off for one reason or another. Then came Bernd Jurgen Brandes, a year younger than Meiwes himself, also a computer professional. The two met in March 2001 at Meiwes' Rotterdam apartment, worked out the plan for the slaughter, and even for the taping of it. The deed was done in a room built for this purpose, the meat cut up for storage in a freezer for gradual consumption by the advertiser.

Months later, another ad of similar content followed, raising public suspicion of its source, and helping police bring the case to the court on charges of cannibalism. Seated before the judge, Meiwes appeared unruffled, smiling and talking with his lawyer. He confessed to having had a fantasy, as early as twelve years old, of having a good looking, younger brother whom he would keep with himself by killing and eating him. He claimed that his victim in the realized fantasy had volunteered to serve his wish, and that there was neither force nor any surprise in the matter. The German court sentenced Meiwes to eight and a half years in prison in 2007. That was how far it went.

Yes, the incident possibly made many too numb to comment on it. It did not, however, seem to have affected Europe much. But common sense makes one marvel at the reality of two educated, adult professionals: one announcing a brutish fantasy and another offering to be its fulfillment.

Story #19
The Treeshade Wish

I used to see a retired gentleman sitting in the portico of his suburban home every evening on my daily walk. He was often alone, although he lived with his family and was attended to as needed. He was well known where he lived, and in many cities far beyond, as a pioneer missionary. I never met him face to face; perhaps I should have.

What makes him memorable is what I had heard of him as a youth. His parents disapproved of his association with a small holiness movement in his hometown that preached deeper personal spirituality and practiced simple living, somewhat like the Amish or the Puritans among the early American settlers. The parents gave him the proverbial option of "our way or the highway," and he chose the latter.

With all his earthly belongings including a vernacular Bible in a single cloth bag slung on his shoulder, he journeyed barefoot to the state capital about a hundred miles to the south. No one was expecting him there, but that was the direction he chose. Several days passed before he made it to the outskirts of the city. By then his feet were swollen and heavy. He sat exhausted under a shade tree. In a cracking voice he groaned, "Lord, I wish I had a place somewhere here to lay my head."

That exact spot where he sat became his future street address. That was where I saw him sitting, facing the wall. Within yards of the old shade tree was a large piece of property which his sons had bought for him as they themselves became men of means. Just a wish uttered had become a granted estate.

Story #20
The Challenged Lion

I was in a gathering where a well-traveled entrepreneur recalled his visit to a South African wildlife park. He and his team had their tickets for the guided tour of the park, but they were turned away because of an emergency closing. The dominant lion of a pride, he said, had been challenged by four of his own sons. The scene of fierce rage between the two sides was too dreadful for human presence. When the tour party was allowed reentry the following day, they learned that the chase had gone as far as sixty miles through the forest preserve, where the dominant lion was killed by the sons. "I think he was defeated only psychologically," the gentleman commented.

What happened to the parent lion sounded much like the many heart-rending scenarios of human families, too. The great Moghul emperor Shah Jahan was shut away in house arrest by his own son, Aurangzeb, who even disallowed him the funeral that was customary for emperors. Consider the pain of Eli or Samuel who were de facto rulers of their people, but not of their rebellious sons.

The heroic King David himself fared no better; he became a fugitive in his own kingdom when his charming son Absalom staged a coup and displayed his carnal liberties with David's concubines in public view. It takes hardly any physical force to undo a parent.

Story #21
The Skyhigh Strip

Term limit and loss of rank threaten even so-called heavenly bodies. A new victim of such dishonor is Pluto, the outermost planet of the solar system. He appeared in the solar birth register in 1930, and most of the twentieth century had been happy with his place in the family. From ancient times, his namesake has been a god of a major afterlife department—death and the aftermath. Many cultures have him in their mythologies, and so, have huge temples built for him. In cultures where he is personally not present, he has his counterparts held in no less esteem.

All that has changed. The International Astronomical Union of Paris has determined that Pluto has glowed enough with his betters, undeservedly. They have therefore demoted him to the rank of a dwarf planet, worthy of little more than a ghetto of over 136,500 minor planets. He will have a mere ID number hereafter: 134340.

Some comfort remains for Pluto, however. He is not without loyalists. Dissenting astronomers have a campaign going for him. They contend that the "dwarf planet" definition is unscientific and the decision on this status change is undemocratic.

Pluto's plight is a cosmic joke, it seems. Pluto was what it was before 1930 and it continues as what it was meant to be, even after this title-strip. Promises of position or power that people give or take stay or go as times change. Nations rewrite histories or even the scriptures of others for advantages in argument. People once praised as heroes, prophets or inventors have been disgraced, some with persuasive reasons, and many without.

The truth perhaps is that we are not able even to name a thing right, much less understand it.

Story #22
At Magma's Mercy

It will be another four hundred years, say the experts, before we see a hurricane of the deadly force of Katrina. Let us hope so, but when it did strike in 2005, New Orleans alone lost over 1,800 lives and $100 billion worth of property. The city lay flooded for weeks, displacing over a million people. Passionate debate followed the disaster for the rebuilding of the city, on the same site, starting with congressional funds of nearly $150 billion.

Political debates seldom reveal that the city had advance warnings of its perilous state. Scientists, including geologists at the University of New Orleans itself, had shown that New Orleans is sinking a few inches every year. In fifty years or less, they say, the sinking of the city will be complete. The soft, silt ground of the "Big Easy" is slowly giving way to the rising sea level. Politics still favors its rebuilding.

New Orleans is not alone with a future of dread. Take a handful of cities across the globe: Tokyo, Hong Kong, San Francisco, Los Angeles, Tehran, Mumbai, or Ankara.

Each has had massive human toll and loss of wealth by earthquakes. Still, in their glittering sky views built over the quake debris, landmark business towers flourish. Some of them spin more money in a single day than many small nations can in a whole year. Perhaps your pensions, stocks and securities live in one or more of them.

Isn't it ironic that these great structures stand on sliding plates of earth, over the fickle fluid beneath the surface? Minor movements of the earth's plates crumble the surface and whatever stands upon it. For most cities it is not whether it would happen, but when.

If my future is in the hands of a business house which stands tall on a sliding stack of brittle plates resting upon mere gummy matter, I deserve pity. The way life runs its show, the insurer himself needs an insurer, the banker a greater banker, the treasury yet another treasury. That plan can work only if the greater insurer would not need a still greater one; the greater banker should face no threats of bankruptcy; the greater treasury should be one where neither thieves nor moth have entry. If these conditions fail, I will be at magma's mercy. Every tower that did not rise from the Rock of Ages is little more than a stick figure in a child's game in the sandy soil.

Story #23
Particle Arrangement

In a clinic's waiting room, a mother apologized to us for her baby's diaper accident. Among those in the room were my friend James, a PhD in Organic Chemistry, and I. Being a reflective thinker and a man of sympathetic understanding, James, true to his nature, said quietly, "The mother of that baby doesn't have to be embarrassed. The bowel movement is the completion of a chemical action in the body. What the body empties out is unpleasant to our senses merely because of the way chemicals are arranged in it. Just change the order of the chemical arrangement in it—the result will be a product of appeal, even of fragrance."

What James said made me think of the supposed foulness of things. Anything gone awry or foul is only an altered mode of the original. All the foul words we may speak or write are merely from the selective use of characters or sounds. A greeting, a love note, a cheering sound, a swear word, a ransom note, a genocide slogan, all come from the same alphabet arranged or rearranged. One site of the Internet gives the antidote for snakebite, while another takes one to a snake pit. A message of care goes from a parent to a child; a prayer flies heavenward from one's penitent lips; an eviction note makes a single mother and her children homeless; a phone text announces a lost child's return. All of these happen with the arrangement of the twenty-six characters of the alphabet for the English world, twenty-eight in Arabic, twenty-two characters for the Hebrew world, or a similar handful in any other.

Paracelsus said that all things are poisonous except for the measure and proportion. Poet John Donne says all human passions, even the hell-bent, could reverse to undo their native evil. A greedy man with God in him turns the greed for the good he just found in God. Another man given to habitual rage can use that very passion against the threat to purity. A man of lust would shun his ways, but its power could reset as devotion; rebellion could reverse itself as self-giving. In each instance, the power to hurt is altered.

We have the limitless strength to undo life or the angelic means to elevate it.

Story #24
Views of a Fall

E mperor Julian made himself quite sensational in power. The successor to Christian rulers, Julian wanted paganism as his state religion. He spoke, wrote and decreed fiercely against the Christian population of the Roman empire of his eighteen-month reign. Julian believed that he was the reincarnation of Alexander the Great. His mentor Maximus of Ephesus convinced Julian by prophecy that he was destined to restore paganism in the empire.

Once in power, Julian titled himself Pontifex Maximus, according to the Church's model itself, and got busy switching the present with the past. Pagan temples reopened, while church properties were by law closed, at imperial pleasure. The Patrician Guard was purged of Christian personnel. So was the government. Julian's new School Law denied license to Christian faculty. All religions were fine for Julian, including the Jewish, but not "the Galileans," his pejorative for Christians. He even ordered the rebuilding of the Jewish Temple, but surprise earthquakes, lightnings and eruptions of fire on the site prevented the work from proceeding beyond the very start.

Julian set his eyes on Persia for a needless war. Counselors tried to discourage him. No, he would go ahead, and he did. On the way, he stopped in Caesarea where his old college friend Basil was the revered Metropolitan. Somehow Julian sought to be Basil's guest for a meal. The ascetic bishop sent him a dish of barley loaves and radishes, which were his own simple menu. Julian was enraged. He sent the bishop a return gift of a bundle of hay, along with the threat to destroy the city and to remove its people to sheer pasturage as soon as he returned from Persia. The bishop gathered his people at the Cathedral of Didymus on Mt Caesarea for communal prayer, during which he saw a vision of heavenly armies circling the mount, and St. Mercurius, a martyr of Decian persecution, fighting on his behalf. In Persia, at that very moment, a soldier's arrow struck Julian's liver. It took his life.

That same day, Didymus the Blind of Alexandria, an eighty-five-year-old sage of great renown whom even Julian's admirers praised in their writings, was sitting in his chair. Not having eaten anything all day, he fell asleep and had a dream of white horses running in different directions, and their riders crying out, "Tell Didymus, 'today, at the seventh hour, Julian died; arise and eat, and inform Athanasius the bishop, that he may also know it.'" Didymus noted the time and confirmed the event.

According to an apocryphal record, Julian at his death said, *"Visciti, Galilae!"* meaning, "Thou hast conquered, O, Galilean!"

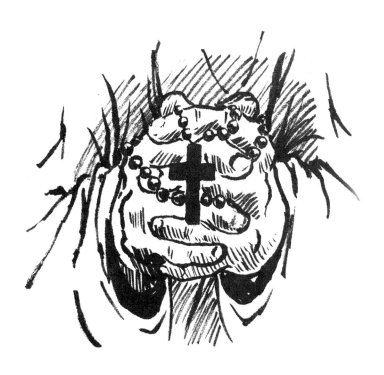

Story #25
The Slow-Witted Saint

A t the age of twenty, the peasant youth Jean-Marie Vianney enrolled for clerical training in a French seminary. Barely average at best, his study skills impressed none. He had the unflattering privilege of sitting with the little teens for his classes, where he ranked as the last and the least. Latin was a core subject, which was dreadfully difficult for him. Mathias Loras, a twelve-year old but the brightest classmate, was assigned to help him, but to no avail. One day, frustrated by the doltish peer's slowness, Mathias boxed his ears in front of all the rest. Rather than return the blow to defend his honor, Vianney fell at the feet of Mathias Loras, asking for forgiveness. Instantly in their tearful embrace, the two bonded for life from that moment on.

Vianney still struggled in learning. In fact, the school had to let him switch his readings from Latin to French. His teachers agreed that his zeal offset his weakness in learning. At age twenty-nine, Vianney was ordained with understandable reservation and given charge of the rural parish of Ars in France as an assistant to the vicar. The superiors debated if he should ever be given the duties of hearing confession. The French Revolution had just run its course, so religion was nearly wiped out from the nation, it seemed. So, Vianney and the people who sent him to Ars had little worry.

Well, surprises come as they always do. Few knew that Vianney was a lightning rod, the kind you can't advertise for. Deep, inner fires of purity and prayer were his signature strengths since childhood. Strong emotional intelligence drew people toward him. He counseled people one by one to right living and wholeness. Within a few years of his charge as Cure d'Ars, the entire city reversed its manner of thinking and living. As a confessor, he attracted penitents every day from all over France, the wider Europe, and even the US, with hundreds willing to wait their turn for a few minutes with him. Often a casual word of his or a moment of prayer with him would result in miraculous outcomes. He had a supernatural understanding of people, often revealing their past and their future. At least 20,000 people visited him per year personally, while the audiences of his sermons rose to 100,000 in his latter days—-all this in a place that had been cleansed of religion. The world came to hear a man who owned nothing and sought nothing except the power of deeper prayer life. A century and a half later, the very man thought to be of mulish wit, stands canonized as St. John Vianney, and declared the model for clergy, even for the learned.

So much for screening and rating.

Story #26
The Graceful Curve

H. G. Wells writes of one Dr. Moreau, the cold-hearted scientist who comes to an island in the South Seas for his experiments in biology. He surgically alters the island's animals with human traits, his goal being the creation of a species of his own fancy. The wolf, the leopard, the puma, the ape, the rabbit of the island are all his victims, all turning into unsightly forms, half human and half brute. These "Beast People" lost whatever was naturally lovely in them. Their altered forms displayed unequal length of legs, "forearms hanging weakly to the side," a "forward carriage of the head," and similar oddities. In particular, Wells notes that the Ape-Man "lacked that inward sinuous curve which makes the human figure so graceful."

A curve, rather than a beam—-that's the beauty of the human spine—-at least one aspect of it. It gives the body the delicate ability of its pleasing measures of movement. The power of the delicate is often the ultimate strength of humans, nay, even all living beings.

The instinct to bow the head or to bend the knee, to give or to receive mercy with a brimful eye, to utter the kindly word that heals by its landing, to sound a note that lifts the soul, are all delicate motions of the soul on which even the highest of strengths depends.

Solomon speaks of the unarmed wise old man turning away an invading army by the mere tenderness of his wisdom. Salar Jung, the great collector of the world's best art, snapped at another collector's presumptuous offer of any price for modesty sculpted in Benzoni's masterpiece, "The Veiled Rebecca." That little inward curve that few may see is the best mark of the Creator's touch on your frame.

Story #27
The Zimbabwe Dollar

"Two hundred trillion dollars for a loaf of bread—take it or leave it. It's sure to be higher tomorrow," reported *The Times* of London, on how prices of grocery ran in Zimbabwe in 2009. How about a two-liter bottle of cooking oil? Five billion Zimbabwe dollars, the same amount that a "low income" worker earned in monthly wages in the country. How about a pint of milk? Three billion dollars, or 30 US cents. Professor Steve Hankey of Johns Hopkins University graphed Zimbabwe's inflation hitting 79,600,000,000%, seventy-nine billion plus, that is. That's not all; even these dreadful prices kept doubling every 24.7 hours. Between 2008-2009, the billion-denomination proved too small, and the trillions rolled in. By the way, 1.2 trillion Zimbabwean dollars would buy one British pound. As the year 2009 ended, the Z-dollar, no matter of what range, was worth nothing. As of June 2015, the Z-dollar has finished out its career. Long lines of customers at Z banks were turning in their native currency for a few US dollars or South African

Rands. The exchange rate: 175 quadrillion Z dollars--that is fifteen zeros after 175—for US$5.00

Hyperinflation of this kind zaps out an economy at fatal speed. No pretense of strength stops its devouring power. Zimbabwe printed worthless paper money to pay its bills, but without value back up, paper is pulp fiction. The claim of face value is as large a lie as the trillion-dollar digit trail.

Not unlike the "Z lesson" is the credit front of Wall Street tycoons or powerhouses. Great were the falls of many a business house when its boasts were tested. It happens even to places of learning or religion. Their beliefs sound well-spelt, their titles parade well, but their starving soul dies hearing its own dirge. Prophet Isaiah condemns people who idly mouth words of dead tradition, when their hearts are far from God. Zimbabwe's money may be unmade or remade, but a soul parting company with its maker voids itself.

Story #28
The Shape of Value

It was a long time ago that I first landed at JFK, entering the US. I can't say that I had a great deal of culture shock, but within minutes I had my first tricky moment. I was supposed to call a friend in Texas with my onward flight information. Straight past the customs doors I saw a bay of pay phones and a fast-moving line heading toward each. I took my place in one, with a handful of coins in one hand, and a suitcase in the other. A quarter was all it took for a call, but I wasn't sure which coin was the quarter. The man behind me said, "Take two of these, and one of these," identifying two dimes and a nickel. Well, the nickel, for some reason, was larger than the dime, and I asked the man if he had the order backward. "No," he said, "two of these and one of these should do it." This guy could be trying to pull a fast one on me for an easy laugh, I thought. So, with great prudence I turned with the same question to the next man, as quietly as I could. He too said the same thing. I eyed the first man and this new fellow quickly, thinking they had exchanged a wink or a nod about me.

That did not seem to be the case. However, I wasn't going to be hoodwinked, I decided, and I walked over to a lady at a service desk. I put my handful of coins on her table and asked if she would let me make a collect call to Texas. She gladly gave me the phone, without charge. I made my call, and soon I was on my four-hour flight to DFW.

On the way I began to reflect on the puzzle I had faced over shapes and values. By mere chance I noticed the dollar bills I had on me: the ones, the fives, tens, twenties, even the hundreds, all were of the same size, in color and details, except for the value part. It just struck me then: size did not matter at all; the seal and signature alone did. "Whose image and superscription do you see on your coin?", Jesus asked the scheming Pharisees who questioned him on the rightness of Jews paying taxes to the Romans.

They answered, "Caesar's."

Then "give to Caesar what is due unto him, and to God what is due unto him," he said to them.

It may not be far-fetched to say that humans are coins of God, combining his image and value imprint. One's entire life is but a tenure of currency as a coin authorized by the King's image and superscription.

Story #29
The Asimov Ego

Science fiction author Isaac Asimov has published over five hundred books, reputedly covering most of the categories of the Dewey decimal system. He is known to have claimed that only two men were smarter than he: astronomer Carl Sagan and computer scientist Marvin Minsky. Interesting.

There need be little hurry in checking out these claims.

One wonders why other great thinkers or writers elsewhere have forgone their arguable bragging rights. Aristotle wrote over three hundred books, it is said, possibly fitting more categories of library classification, but we have only ten of them surviving, nonetheless, great works. Aristotle could well be glad that he is dead and had not made any grandiose claims about his own brain power, because we now know of the many errors in his works.

Augustine of Hippo, who wrote over five million words in over a hundred books, only laments the depth of his ignorance. Albert the Great and Thomas Aquinas, master and disciple respectively, were authors of encyclopedic range and depth, yet said little about themselves. At the Council of Trent, the Roman Catholic Church placed the Bible and Aquinas' *Summa* on the altar, about which philosopher Jack Maritain says, "greater honor no man has." Yet, the *Summa* is an incomplete work because Aquinas, after a mystical experience, said that all that he had written seemed like straw.

Pascal said that humans have two forms of ignorance: one is the natural ignorance, which everyone tries to remove little by little through learning. The other is the wise ignorance which knows itself, which only the enlightened minds have. Sounds as though the best we may learn from learning is how vast our ignorance is.

Story #30
The Cast of Faith

I just read about the American spouse of an Indian Hindu being denied entrance to Hindu temple grounds in North India. Foreigners of non-Asian hue or even natives of other faiths being turned away from temple premises is hardly news on the subcontinent. However, this couple was fretting and fuming. Their protests resulted in physical assault on the husband and police action afterwards. The police could do little, so the matter went on to the US Embassy.

Incidentally, even a central cabinet minister of India was told not to let his wife of non-Hindu heritage accompany him to the temple. Well, many non-Hindus do enter many a temple every day, just by playing the part. Evidently, that trick doesn't work for people of give-away skin tones.

More striking is the widely known story of a singer of national renown, a former Catholic, now a devout Hindu. His talented singing of temple devotionals endears him to the devotees, but his caste disqualified him for entry into the temple's worship quarters. He would therefore arrange private services by Hindu priests, which the media has often covered. This, by the way, is in a former princely state whose last monarch's claim to fame rests on his decree to grant the privilege of temple entry even to the Untouchables.

One might say that a deity which has worshipers thronging regardless of prohibitions is in a pretty advantageous position. However, these deities themselves are not free from their own political or personal worries. War gods with unsettled issues of past disputes are concerned about their own security; goddesses of undying jealousies, seduced or raped and suffering the consequences of the nightlife of male gods, have new vengeance programs; gods upset at loyalty shifts of peers or humans have their own problem-ridden justice projects; stories of gods with food addictions, say, incurable weakness for sweets, liquor, butter, oil, and what not, fill up the mythological gossip stands. The census of such gods, most of them unknown beyond a village or two, far outnumber the humans of their worship territories.

Perhaps the offense of temple entry should go to the presiding deity of the place himself or herself rather than to the police, the court, or the embassy. An old time Jewish farmer settled a case of this kind by that approach. Gideon ben Joash tore down the altar of Baal, a competing cult god in Israel. A mob of his own people rose in riot, demanding Gideon's life for the deed. "If Baal be a god, let him look to his own business," Gideon's father said to the madding crowd. That word prevailed.

Story #31
Love by Law

Right after the fatal car crash of Princess Diana, seven of the menacing paparazzi were charged with the violation of the Good Samaritan Law. These men took all the shots they needed and left the scene after one of them also had felt the pulse of the dying princess, still without extending any possible help. In Europe and America, the law requires that an accident witness lend all possible help to the victim. Its violation is punishable in France by up to $100,000.

My title for this story alludes to the biblical parable of the Good Samaritan in which an outsider rescues a waylaid Jew, injured by robbers. The Samaritan takes the wounded man to the nearest inn, spares no effort or expense, and even promises to return to cover any charges still outstanding. The Samaritan does this as no duty under law, but out of love for a complete stranger.

That should help us see how good laws come about. Every good law shows the genius and virtue of a good lawmaker. Much of the world has borrowed heavily from

Moses, the Lawgiver. Moses did not create the Law, but only recorded and delivered it at God's command. The Ten Commandments are part of it. See what they call for: worship only the true God; keep the Sabbath; respect your parents; do not kill; do not commit adultery; do not covet, and so on. Each of them ensures some universal virtue. Now consider some of their extended texts: do not reap from the edges of your field, but leave them for the needy stranger in your land; do not enlist a newly married man for military duty for the first year, but let him be with his new bride; do not cook the meat of the lamb in its mother's milk; do not charge interest on a loan to your brother; set a slave free in the seventh year, and so on. Each of these laws is inspired by love for its users. It would be something like a parent instructing an older child to take care of his younger siblings.

Some say the Old Testament is harsh, but Jesus taught that its entire bulk crystallizes into two precepts: Love the Lord God with all your heart, all your mind and all your body. Second, love your neighbor as you would love yourself. To further validate it, he said, "I have come not to remove the Law, but to fulfill it." If so, both the Law and Love are twins of the same parent. Love can never be lawless, nor can good law be loveless.

Story #32
Dwarfs Serving Turns

J ust like us, stars too must age and die. The estimated size of our universe, the galaxies of our neighborhood, and even the little solar system, keeps growing day by day. The Milky Way, our home base, has 200-400 billion stars, our own sun being just average sized. Once a star uses up its nuclear power that produces energy, it shrinks in size to a dwarf, first white, and then black. Much of its outer material shed, the dwarf burns on for billions, possibly trillions more years before it cools, and becomes a planet-size diamond!

A few trillion years, and you have an entire diamond island. Not just one, but billions of them, if every sun has a similar fate. How's that for a wait? Science marks this universe's birth somewhere around 14 billion years ago. Even if there is a star collapsing right now and shrinking and cooling off as a result, the time needed for the predicted product is insanely long.

Isn't science asking us to believe or to have faith in things that exist not yet, as though they do? None has ever seen a black dwarf. If it could be found and reached, earth people would start the diamond drill. Wait a minute: if galaxies are to shed billions of dead stars in the form of whole diamonds, wouldn't that be a cosmic joke on our present craze for so-called precious metals and stones?

Story #33
The Bullet Fee

T he historic student protests in the Tiananmen Square of the Chinese capital were merely for minimal human liberties in a society which lives under brutal force. In total contempt of popular sentiments, the government seemed to say, "do or die." Tanks rolled right over the protesting students, grinding their bodies to the paved grounds. Many were shot point blank. News stories said that one victim's family received a charge of 11 cents toward the cost of the single bullet that killed their son.

The 11 cents of China is a bargain compared to a similar state demand of a poor Iranian family twenty years later. Consider the story of Kaveh Alipour, an Iranian youth of nineteen, in the June 23, 2009 issue of *The Wall Street Journal*. The Iranian security forces shot and killed this student of Drama at a traffic crossing. The family located the body in a Tehran morgue two days later, with no help from the state. Instead, the state demanded $3,000 as a "bullet fee" from Kaveh's father, a poor doorman at a clinic. His entire net worth was less than the assessed fee for the bullet. He appealed for consideration, at least as a veteran of the Iran-Iraq War. The appeal was granted on the condition that the body would not be buried in Tehran, nor would a funeral be held there. They had to take the body to another city where some relatives lived. The slain youth was to have been a groom within a week.

The ideal state is intended to be a family for every citizen, and the ruler of that state, the parent or guardian. Any home that kills its own offspring in the name of law has received its law from either the wrong lawgiver or has become a law unto itself. Dirt-poor states have had rulers listed among the world's richest while their people live like Stone Age primitives. The ruler's word is the only law of such places, hardly with any comfort in it for those who need it most.

Story #34
The Water Man

In the South Indian suburb of a state capital, I once came across a man in his sixties, always well-dressed and of a cheerful face, warmly waving to people as he walked along. Whenever I saw him, he was either coming home from a long-distance trip or heading out on one. What was taking him places?

It turned out that he was a water diviner. When people had building projects, they would start construction only after locating sources of drinking water at the site. Even in places with city water supply, due to its unreliability, a dependable well was a necessity. So, people would hire this gentleman for a day or two. As he walked the grounds, his body would sense water tables at certain locations. He would tap the spot for flagging, and then go on to one or two more. Only after digging at the choice spot and finding water would his clients begin construction.

He was a remarkably fortunate man, living fairly well at a time - long before modern days of digitally generated wealth - when thirty percent unemployment was normal.

The privilege of steady work is not exclusive to the water diviner. Not one lands on this planet without a signature gift or skill to live by. The singer does not have to invent the voice, though she may train. The marksman has an innate ability to be accurate. An architect visualizes shapes, a fisherman rides the wave, and each tradesman plies his ware. A natural ease accompanies each innate talent. This waterman seemed to surpass them all with a golden precept: Out of a man of faith "shall proceed rivers of life." His arrival promises new streams in dry dust and apparently rocky ground.

Story #35
The Spider's Chide

A team of Swedish scientists showed that a spider can exert 172 times its body weight on an object. In human terms that would be like one person turning himself into a small army of 172.

Well, the spider is not the singular wonder of animal strength. Just about every creature has some peculiar power boast. Snapping turtles bite with a force of over a thousand pounds, no less than tigers and hyenas. A June beetle, according to *Scientific American,* can hold its weight sixty-six times in equilibrium, while a horse cannot balance even its own weight. The beetle, scientists say, can escape from under a piece of cardboard one hundred times its weight, using its head and legs as levers. A tiny flea can jump two hundred times its own body length. And the list could go on.

We marvel at Genghis Khan's empire: with merely a hundred thousand soldiers he created an empire over one-third of the globe in an era when medieval limits were a convenient excuse for thousands of petty princes to stay petty. Khan had no aviation, no telecommunications, not even bullets. Horses were the speediest means of movement to connect one end of his world with another. His empire was the result of the human equivalent of spider power.

But the power of the Spirit is the greatest creative capacity in humans, and it is shockingly underused. In the spiritual world, which is barred to none, Jesus said, one could speak by faith to a mountain to command its removal, and it should happen. Not by might, nor by power, but my Spirit, reminds Prophet Zechariah of God's work with humans. We go to bed with untold amounts of unused power. When we rise in the morning with no better action plan, shouldn't the spider chide us?

Story #36
The Harvest of Hunger

The San Bushmen of South Africa have the power of a paradox in their native soil, and they may perhaps become rich by it. Growing in the blazing heat of their desert terrain is *hoodiya*, an ugly, cactus-like plant which, if ingested, staves off hunger with no discomfort or side effects. The plant had always been well in used in the land, but none ever thought much about it, at least until now.

It is said that while the bushmen go hunting, they chew a little bit of the *hoodiya*, which saves them the bother of packing any food for their way up and down. Researchers say that hoodia has a molecule in it that fools the taster's brain into thinking that his stomach is full. BBC Newsmen who sampled "half a banana size" of the plant felt no hunger at all even after a four-hour drive. So, they went straight to bed without supper and rose next morning, skipping breakfast, and at lunch forced themselves to eat just because they thought they should eat, but still feeling no need for food at all.

Now *hoodiya* has been discovered by the rest of the world. And the whole world wants all of the *hoodiya* that the bushmen can harvest. *Hoodiya* will reshape the obese crowds of the West. Companies have already started the work on marketing this giant revenue maker. It will feed and rebuild the tribes of the West's hungry hunters in a new way and bring home for them the ultimate game.

Bread, the staff of life, shuns many and stuffs others. Hunger has driven humanity from one land or shore to another. The overfed fight their own bulk, and hunger must bring its silent strength to win the battle. "Blessed are the hungry, for they shall be fed," begin the great beatitudes. The person who declared it, himself fed the hungry and even showed us where to find our daily bread. It appears he also has given the bush people the means to turn hunger into a source of wealth.

Story #37
The Imitative Animal

Alexandra, the Princess of Wales, walked with a slightly noticeable rheumatoid limp. Not a matter to be disheartened about at all: society ladies all over London soon took to affecting that limp.

Go back a couple of millennia, where we have a similar quirk in the case of Alexander the Great. The young emperor had a wry neck. All his courtiers thought it proper to have their necks tilted a bit to one side, until there were scarcely any straight necks to be found in royal circles. At some point Alexander had enough of it and landed a blow on one of his tilt-neck courtiers. The effect was instantaneous. All court necks straightened as if by a single jolt.

The whole history of fashions runs this way. Richard Steele writes of war injuries and walking sticks being the hottest trends of style right after a war. Matted hair, pierced body parts, tattooed skin, cords, thick threads, strung beads, and similar attire have often been caricatures of wandering gypsies or idle almsmen in olden times. The last two decades have shown how youth culture has turned these into trendy industries.

Humans are the most imitative of all animals. They learn by imitation. They create cultures by imitation and preserve them by the same means. The stage and the statecraft set the popular speech patterns of the land, insisting on their correct imitation. Companies recruit graduates of name-brand universities hoping that these graduates have learned to imitate the best brains in the world.

So, here's the catch: imitation can result in ridicule, or it can result in reward. It is all a matter of who or what one imitates. The Apostle Paul urged us to "be imitators of Christ," knowing that none could regret the result. Thomas à Kempis signed on to that idea, and it gave him the material for authoring the great medieval classic, *The Imitation of Christ.*

Story #38
The Dignity of Begging

A national daily in a developing nation once had a cartoon of two of its corrupt politicians chatting in front of a world map on the wall. With a pointer in hand, one touched a tiny black dot in the middle of the Pacific Ocean and asked his colleague, "How come, my friend, this country hasn't given us any economic aid yet?" The cartoon easily made the point of the national disgrace of going a-begging among world nations.

A "poor relation," says Charles Lamb, himself having been poor, "is a preposterous shadow, known by its length in the noontide of our prosperity. He is known by his knock." Whether it is a person or a nation, the visit of this kind is seldom desired or awaited.

Now consider another visitor, who also knocks, but with pleasing results. In Vedic schools, in desert communities of early Christians, in monastic institutions, dedicated young people came, falling prostrate before the masters, begging to be accepted as disciples. If received, the seeker considered it a great honor.

No one has been despised for being a beggar for knowledge.

Another kind of begging defies all rational thinking: begging in prayer. With accents of personal experience, poet George Herbert speaks of it thus:

> Thou hast given so much to me
> Give me one thing more, a grateful heart.
> See how thy beggar works on thee
> By art.

> ("Gratefulness": 1-4.)

This is a pious man amusing himself in his role as a beggar who is richly favored, still at it for more from God. If so, the mightiest of the godly people we know, Moses, Elijah, Peter, Teresa of Avila, or Sadhu Sundar Singh, were beggars of a high order. They only received in order to give away. They also stood between the living and the dead, simply by the power they had with God, yet their power came from begging. They model a begging that exalts the beggar.

Story #39
Confessed Conquests

David Pattom, a South Indian retreat leader, got a call from a lady asking to be confessed. Sensing a peculiar urgency in the request, the priest agreed, and the lady arrived within the hour. To his shock, the priest saw the body of the woman covered with boils, head to foot, the pus oozing, and even dripping. She said she could neither kneel nor sit, but only stand in the confessional. He agreed. The smell from the body of the woman was such that would come out of putrid flesh. The confession took about nine minutes. Before dismissing her, he wanted to lay hand on the woman and pray but recoiled at the thought of touching her. Instantly he heard a voice within: "What you have done unto the least of these, you have done for me; what you have not done unto the least of these, you have not done for me." Not another moment lost, the priest put his hand upon the woman's head, prayed for her, and sent her away with his blessing.

Three days later the priest received a call from her to say that the boils had begun to fade, the flow of pus having ceased. In another call seven days later, she said that her body was entirely free of the boils. I wonder if this woman had any knowledge of what ancient Jews had to do if they had an infectious disease. The Book of Leviticus requires that a skin infection be reported to the priest, who may quarantine the individual first and then provide ritual cleansing, before certifying the patient's restored wellness. Not entirely unlike the Levitical priest, this confessor led this lady from illness to wellness. For her own part, the woman initiated her own healing, starting with her own inner springs. It seems that a great many of our maladies should give way to the sacred impulse of confessing our inner corruption. A pharmacy may hold the salve for some physical ills. The Paraclete holds the salve for the whole person.

Story #40
Elective Misery

There was a rural town bemoaned for its dire poverty. In the middle of the town was a church that could not show, among its members, a single home that could claim a steady means of livelihood. The bishop of the district, much concerned about this place and its people, found a middle-aged priest willing to go to this parish as its minister. The villagers were not particularly crazy about the church or its religious services. The priest's coming did not excite the people, and he did not need to be told so. Still, he had a good number of people gathering on his first Sunday. They had come as a matter of habit, expecting little more than the routine motions.

In the middle of the service, the priest used the time allotted for the homily merely to introduce himself and to thank them for welcoming him as their vicar. He told them that their economic hardships worried him. Sympathy soothes, but it doesn't buy food, they thought.

Then he said something that gave them a gentle jolt. "The bishop has sent me here with a large sum of money for you."

None of them was sure if it meant money for each person. "I said, I have come to you with a lot of money," the priest repeated more forcefully, and the people kept staring as if to say, "Yes, go on, we're listening!"

Apparently wanting a still stronger sign that his message was reaching them, he said even more emphatically, "I say, I have come to you with a lot of money, for every one of you." By now it sounded too good to be true. Before he might lose them, he added, "No, it won't simply be passed around in a plate. Convince me that you need it, and you shall have your portion."

The priest was not bluffing. He had a big plan for rural self-employment. His main project was a poultry farm. Each family could take a certain number of chickens on credit and pay for them out of the sale of eggs or the meat. There was no limit to the number they could order. Each family could set its own income goal and get going with it. Many of the parish homes prospered by the plan, but some did not, for one reason or another. Of course, we never lack a reason for things not working.

As a teacher I have told my classes that *I am* that priest. I want my students to be superior performers, each one earning an A. The offer is open, and I mean what I say. The goal is realistic, and I can help it happen. I'm afraid some students needlessly settle for lower goals, but there are a number who reach out for the top spots – and achieve their dreams.

No village needs to starve where the principles of success are at work. Humans have bleak times, but they can usually be bettered. If I were to follow the logic of the priest's homily, our poverty, for the most part, would be elective. Why would I not want to better myself, if help itself is begging for its use?

Story #41
The River Ride to Riches

S ome smart people announce their seminars on how to make a lot of money and make it fast! Usually, it works for the presenters only. For a change, here is a sure-win tip for you, and there is no charge.

The Genesis story of creation says that a river of four fountainheads took four directions from the Garden of Eden. Pison, the first, flowed toward Havilah, known for the finest gold and precious stones. Gihon, the next, ran to the land of Cush, and Hiddekel to Assyria, the evident agent of fertility for territories. Euphrates, the fourth river, though left with the mere mention of its name, has cradled empires. Modern maps help little in telling us more of these lands and their waters in the world preceding the Great Flood.

"Okay, that's fine, but show me the money," you say. Did you notice that the Pison circles Havilah's gold? Many nations have lived in poverty, while owning untouched gold and gems beneath their land surface. Apparently, our predecessors made the best of Havilah's geology, and we are yet to locate their helpful records. If our big corporations knew exactly where Havilah was, perhaps excavations could start for its gold this very day.

Forget the gold for a moment. Merely following an earthly river in itself is a move of gain. Civilizations develop along the landscapes carved out by rivers. Where a river or a stream enters, life and riches also enter. A river causes strings of cities to spring up along its course. Mark the wealth of each such city and see what we owe to the river's way. The riverheads of Eden, like anything else from God, were not meant for a single race or nation alone. They chose diverse courses, as bidden. What is the use of a great river if it only coils around a little town? Likewise, of what use is a god if he is solely god of a mountain, a tree, a shrine, a lake and so on?

The springs of Eden outrun the currents of trade and culture. By default, Pison always heads toward riches, but its greater service is to remind us of its origin. It says, only one thing is necessary: choose the King's course. Riches are strewn along the way for their right use. Why then sit by the rivers of Babylon, weeping?

Story #42
The Rewrite Ride

Two thousand insurance adjustors arrived in Florida to process the damage claims of Hurricane Charlie. Though not the most bitterly remembered of American hurricanes, Charlie tore through the Atlantic coast, leaving a ruin trail of $16 billion in property loss and $20 billion to the state's economy.

The insurance folk wanted government certificates of property locations from their owners. Officials could not determine where the houses had stood, because all of them had been crushed into piles of debris. All known landmarks were wiped out. Even the streets were untraceable. The earth seemed to have disowned its children.

Pascal said that what we call our own is so merely by tradition. What we stake out as our own can be overruled by a single stroke of nature. The 2011 tsunami of Japan reportedly moved the whole of Japan ten feet Westward, taking away some of its land mass in the process. The Medes had a proverbial brag about their laws being immutable. That law and even their land itself have been blown away by the storms of time.

Story #43
The Pain of the Painless

The highly honored orthopedic surgeon Paul Brand was once trying to open a large, rusted door lock. He kept turning it until his fingers gave in, but the key did not move. A twelve-year-old boy watching the doctor's effort offered to help. Within seconds he had the lock open.

Intrigued, the doctor observed the lad. The key had cut into the flesh of his fingers and thumb to the bone, but the boy showed no discomfort from it.

That started Dr. Brand's groundbreaking research in leprosy studies. He discovered that leprosy patients lose their extremities to nervous decay, thus killing their sensitivity to pain. He further saw that a leper loses fingers or toes not because bits of them fall off, but because of the heavy wear that goes unregistered by the absence of pain. By this observation, Brand pioneered successful reconstructive surgery for leprosy victims.

Brand wrote later that pain is not the enemy, but the wisdom of the body. Pain tells the body that it hurts for a reason. Without the feeling of pain, one could pick up a red hot horseshoe, take a hard fall, roll over a pile of barbed wire, or swallow liquids scalding hot, yet feel none of the resulting injuries at all. A mother who knew her child had symptoms of insensitivity to physical pain from nervous disorder said she would give anything for her child to have ability to sense pain.

When I read that, I feared that I already have this disorder at a higher level than of the body. My inner man has many times shown signs of personal crassness and utter disregard for the pains of others. Apostle Paul tells the audience of his Roman epistle that all creation groans for the redemption of our bodies. A moment later he says that the Spirit of God himself is groaning within humans for their sake, with utterances too deep for rational understanding. Could it then be an accident that the very act of knowing God personally must start with a pain, the liberating pain of repentance?

Humans face two ironic pain risks: the risk of a broken spirit that is all pain, and the risk of a broken body that feels no pain. Neither is the state of wellness. That's where pain serves as God's minister.

Story #44
What the Doctor Ordered

I fondly recall the many evenings I spent conversing with a medical doctor who shared my interest in Literature. I always felt enriched after a visit with him.

One day we were discussing illnesses and symptoms. "The sign of perfect health in a body is that no part of it would draw attention to itself," he said.

"Wow, what a charming truth!" I said to myself, and have never let it go. We seldom think of our skin unless it itches, or heat or cold affects it. We let the nose just be if the breathing is free. The eye has two million working parts, partakes in 85% of a person's knowledge, processes 36,000 bits of information every hour--yet we hardly think of the eye until a speck of dust falls in it. We give little thought to the 100,000 beats of the heart or to the 2,000 gallons of blood it pumps through the 60,000 miles of blood vessels every day until a discomfort in breathing bothers us.

It is possible to see people who ruin the peace of a home or the decorum of a meeting either because of a hidden gripe or a compulsive need for attention. Once such persons leave, the work gets smoothly done. Good decisions may come in minutes, but a rancorous dispute runs like a cureless ill.

I tend to think that King Solomon, as a lover of peace, pleasure, and beauty, did not like noise or untidiness. The temple that he built is estimated to have cost one trillion dollars in modern money. The person who did the calculations must have factored the noise and cleanliness of the worksite in the cost. According to the record (in the sixth chapter of First Book of Kings – in the Bible), all masonry arrived cut to size, dressed and done! The stones were not small. Average foundation pieces of the period were one meter high and three meters long, no less than a ton, and many of them as heavy as one hundred tons. The king showed that there was no excuse for discord, no matter how great the project was. All it took was for the right part to go to the right space. If one stone did fight the finish, axes would need to swing and chisels strike. That is why the King gave the command that the quarry work be fully done at the source itself - in the sacred halls there was to be no profane sound or sight. If a stone - or, metaphorically, an individual - in the house of worship requires hard dressing and polishing even after having been brought within, does that individual not prove to be an embarrassment and an impediment? Do not such persons draw negative attention to themselves? And who does that help?

Story #45
A Shortsighted Seer

People may think of Jonah as a blundering sailor who didn't need to sail at all. To reach Nineveh, where he was told to go, required only land journey in the opposite direction of Tarshish, the port of his choice. A God-sent storm rocked his ship, alarming all on board. At his request, the ship's crew cast him overboard. Lo, the storm ceased. A submarine of sorts picked him up and cast him ashore. You know what happened after that. Jonah still ends up doing all that he was supposed to do before the story ends. Very good.

Jonah's journey attests to one truth: A ship is always ready to take you away from the right thing. The lure of the port and a convenient ticket just happen to speed up the process. Yet, within minutes of the launch, we regret the embarking.

As a prophet, Jonah is a "seer." Unlike others, he "sees" things long range. However, Jonah's choices are all short range: an excuse voyage to Tarshish, a pretend sleep upon entry, a quick disposal of himself overboard, his mighty pleasure over a one-day vine's shade, and so on. When a long-range man crafts short-range schemes, even Nature rages. Still, from the depths he rises, symbolically enacting a death and resurrection after three days and nights.

Story #46
Don't Worry,
Mama Is Praying

American media knew the Rev. E. V. Hill well. He worked with Martin Luther King, advised national leaders including several presidents, and held an influential pulpit in Los Angeles. Like most African Americans of his time, Hill's beginnings during the Great Depression were extremely humble. Born in a log cabin and raised by a single mother, Hill graduated from his segregated school, with him as its only graduate.

Now it was time to go to college. Of course, there was no money.

He had corresponded with a college in Houston and had received some indication of acceptance, yet somehow the necessary paperwork stood unfinished. At the start of the school year, he decided that he must show up for classes, anyhow. He packed the essentials in an old bag, secured it with a rope around it, and headed out to the bus station with six dollars that his mother had saved up for his education. "Go on, honey, Mama will be praying for you," she said. With brimful eyes, the son left the mother's embrace for his college career. Two dollars went for bus fare, a dollar-and-a-half for a sandwich meal along the way, and the balance was in his pocket. That would be all the money on him as he waited his turn in the registration line at the college. "Not to worry, Mamma is praying," he assured himself.

The line was moving along fast. Hill was behind a dozen or so students. As he drew closer to the counter, Hill heard his heart pounding louder and louder. All he had was the rope-bound bag and the loose change in his pocket. Five more heads in front. Three more. And then came a loud call from behind: "Is there an Ed Hill in this line?" Fearing the worst, Hill answered, "It's me, sir." A man came up and landed his heavy hand on the nervous young man's shoulder, and said, "We've been trying to get a hold of you. A letter we had sent you came back saying the address was wrong. Come with me."

The man Hill followed was the president of the college. At the office he had Hill sign the acceptance of a full-ride scholarship. That was the start of Hill's journey to greatness, along the path the mom in the log cabin saw clearing for her son.

Mothers are major power brokers. They have disabled engines of oppression and altered history. Hagar the slave woman cried in the desert, fearing for the life of her child Ishmael, and the angel's intervention opened her eyes to a spring of fresh water. Jochebed's bassinet for infant Moses bobbed on the Nile until the Pharaoh's daughter ordered it brought to her, only to deliver the child to the rightful bosom for his needed care. Both of them defied the likely death of their offspring.

Story #47
Bridge Yourself

A decade before the Golden Gate Bridge opened in 1937, experts all over the nation had argued against its being built. The reasons advanced were many. The bay was choppy and windy; the waters were five hundred feet deep in the center; the proposed cost of $100 million was an impossible figure for the Depression-strapped economy; alternative funding by bond election would be impossible without the needed backup; the ferry companies and the railroad did not want it; the War department thought it too risky.

Joseph Strauss, a five-foot Chicagoan non-engineer, was determined to move on with the plan, no matter what. He sold the idea to the public and to the powers that be, through an epic campaign. Instead of $100 million, Strauss offered to build it for $35 million, and finished it ahead of schedule and still under budget. The San Francisco Chronicle called the finished product "A thirty-five million dollar steel harp."

"What Nature rent asunder longer ago, man has joined today," said Strauss at its opening, in his exhausted voice. A bridge of 4200 feet removed the "otherness" of people and places surrounding the waters and united them into a magnetic metropolis. As soon as their home grounds touched the edge of the bridge, the residents' status changed. Their properties doubled or tripled in value overnight, and have stayed so ever since.

Bridges are fortune builders, and without them we live marooned. But we have bridges of greater lengths and strengths, buildable other than for travel. Bridges by learning, inventions, friendships, or faith achieve unspeakably larger goals. A peacemaker builds bridges of goodwill to avert conflicts. A scientist or a gifted thinker bridges a need and its answer. Writing to Robert Hooke, his rival, Isaac Newton acknowledged that he had seen what he had only by standing on the shoulders of giants. Moses, Miletus, Confucius, and Chaucer are our reachable helpers by bridges of learning freely built. Bridges of the mind take us to the sages whose wisdom time cannot bury. Far more precious is the gift given to us for bridging with the unfailing, unbreakable truths of eternity.

No man is an island entire of itself, said John Donne. Every man, islander or mainlander, needs a bridge to the eternal city. We are not abandoned on this planet as forlorn beings. Could it be that our estate value is low only because our island lacks a ramp to the bridge?

Story #48
The Future of Old Age

A few years ago, a science magazine featured the picture of an elderly couple on its cover page. Their faces had a gaunt, metallic look. The man was bald, and the woman had pale, limp hair, devoid of even a touch of grace. Though they appeared sturdy and strong, their skin had heavy wrinkles, arranged like a row of tight, round bands. With lips curled in shades of platinum, their eyes fierce and piercing, the pair made a frightening portrait of human lifespan extended, in this case, to 170 years or so. The article about them claimed that life could be extended indefinitely, with consistent maintenance.

Their unsightly longevity worried me. Certainly, they were free to enjoy it if they wished to, but what could they possibly do after the age of eighty or ninety that they had not done until then? They would need to belong to a club of Elective Lifespan People with their own neighborhoods - when millions of people live in every city and most are so lonely, who would worry about a neighbor 170 years old? If these members of the Elective Lifespan club can still operate mentally and physically, how would they keep themselves occupied? There may be some clever answer for each of these questions but let me get to my point.

As flowers of beauty fade, but not without a career of fragrance in the past and a future in their seed, the human body, too, takes leave, having done its work. If this body had no death, we would be condemned to have all our flaws and ills housed in us permanently. The unsightly or the unusable in all of us would fill this planet in very little time. Wouldn't that be hellish misery? If this life is going to transit into a better realm, then preserving the perishing "bonehouse" on this earth is a lowly labor. Conversely, if a better realm is not part of one's future beyond the earth, might settling for a forced stretch on earth be the saddest estate of the soul?

Story #49
Make-Believe Money

Watch the stock market rise and fall. The President appoints a new treasury man, the stock goes a hundred points higher for the day, but not longer. Fed Reserve Chairman speaks in his deliberate obscurity, and the bank rates rattle. If Italy or Greece has debt news in the headlines, the stock sinks, but spikes tomorrow. By such things, no real wealth is added or destroyed anywhere, yet the index creates a storm. The sun still rises as usual, the fish still flit about in the sea, the hills stay green, birds flock and fill the air, and people do what they normally do, except, perhaps, for those who worry about the report. A trillion dollars lost today, but offset tomorrow, presto!

Certainly, we could all understand such storms if an entire harvest is lost, a city is bombed, ships are sunk, or an epidemic spreads. Such things do happen. However, aren't the sliding digital tallies on neon-lit signs quite another matter?

In recent decades we have seen multiple "crashes" of the stock market. Some of the wealthiest persons lost more than half their net worth overnight. The wisdom of Sam Walton on his big loss was charming. He said: "It was paper then, it's paper now." Except that nowadays, it usually isn't even paper.

When money is more fictitious than fiction itself, what power does it have to hurt us? When the whole economy of many nations reeled under the big bust in the housing bubble, the people of Kenya ran their village markets the same way as before. Perhaps they were not networked with the neon money, but they were at least standing on their native ground.

Story #50
Tell Me Who I Am

As I had no experience with large companies at that time, it seemed odd to me when I first heard that a company, struggling to stay afloat, had hired a consultant to help them see what was going wrong. A consultant could be a complete stranger who comes to the firm, very rapidly learns everything he needs to about it, and, when done, gives an assessment of what is right or wrong with a company's operations. Of course, a hefty fee is due for the service.

On reflection, I realized that should not seem strange at all. After all, I do things that are far more difficult to believe. When something is wrong with my stomach, head, or ear, I go to a physician. And what does the doctor do with me? He examines me and gives me an opinion—for a decent fee—and I go by what he says. The body is mine, but a stranger is telling me what I am feeling inside it and why. Should I not know my own body better than a doctor? That rhetorical question may sound perfectly logical, but that is not how life works.

The Greeks had a two-word maxim in their philosophy: *Know Thyself.* The big riddle in the story of Oedipus was for him to discover himself, rather than to show how brilliant he could be in ridding Thebes of its plagues or in finding the murderer of Laius, his father. The truth about ourselves, ironically, is the hardest part of our knowledge search and management.

Story #51
Two Men and Their Widows

When he was about to die, Sisyphus the cunning Greek hero wanted to test the love of his wife. He asked her to leave his body in the open, a matter that incurred the wrath of Pluto, when he reached the underworld. Sisyphus could not believe that his wife would do the unthinkable, whatever his instructions. So, he begged Pluto to let him return to the earth to confront her. No sooner did he see the smile of the earth than his thinking changed. He did not want to go back to Hades as he was supposed to. The sparkle of the sea and the greenery of the earth were worth any risk with Pluto, he thought. Calls, signals, and threats came steadily from Hades, all of which Sisyphus ignored. Finally, Mercury the war god took him back by force to Pluto. In the underworld he was punished with the unceasing task of rolling a huge stone up a steep hill over to the other side. Each time he made it almost to the top, the rock would slip off and roll down to the bottom. Sisyphus would return to the foot of the hill and repeat the attempt, and sadly enough, for the same result. He could not abandon this futile labor, because the gods would not free him from it.

Marxist thinkers often show Sisyphus as their model of the suffering human. As Sisyphus groans under his load, so do all humans under harsh economic systems, they say. They revolt against forced authority and seek to replace it. Some Existentialist philosophers chime in: Sisyphus helps them show how humans can dare even gods, thus scorning their vengeful power.

I wonder why these Existentialists bypassed John Bunyan's Pilgrim who travels toward another world rather than attempt to escape it. He too had a burden, one that had been bound on his back. He climbed in wearying pace to the top of a hill, where stood a cross. As soon as he came to the cross, his burden loosened itself and rolled down, right into a sepulcher, and it was seen no more. His heart was made "glad and lightsome." Later, even his wife and children followed the Pilgrim on the same trail. Reason? The journey's end is in the Kingdom of Light, instead of in Pluto's dark world.

Story #52
The Pearl of Great Price

I t is the traditional pearl-fishing season in the Middle East. Two-men teams launch their simple watercraft into the sea, one man rowing and the other poised for a dive. The diver has a basket dangling on his waist, and a rope tethered to the watercraft. At a certain distance from the shore he jumps, hits the muddy seafloor in seconds, fills up his basket in rapid scoops, and when done, twitches the rope to signal his oarsman friend, who pulls him back up. Back on the shore, they empty the basket and scan the mud load for oysters.

The unsightly oyster is the star and goal of the season. Why? It just might hold a pearl—the proverbial pearl of great price. How? Biology says that a little rub of a sand grain or a similar particle could prick the delicate skin of the oyster. Quickly its body releases a soothing fluid that covers the hurting spot. However, the process does not stop with one coat, two, three, ten or even a hundred. The body fluid, called nacre, brings a soft layer one over the other for, say, three or four years, and by then a symmetrical, shiny bead is formed. The finished product could value from a few dollars to hundreds of dollars or even thousands of dollars. A pearl of Russia's Catherine the Great's jewelry was priced at $600,000, while two pearls of Philip II of Spain's crown were valued at $1.5 million according to early twentieth-century estimates. Well, now you know why people risk their lives and health gathering oysters.

The oyster lives in mire. It ranks low as seafood, supposedly a meat option for the poor, but its injury invests the mighty. Every pearl has a birth story of injury and of lifelong healing. Once harvested, there is no telling how far a journey it has ahead. Traders trail it. Monarchs and powers boast of it. Fortune watchers enrich its lore. A wound takes it from the dirt to the diadem.

Story #53
Shoot before the Strike

Many years ago, I visited an elderly gentleman. An unprotected look at the solar eclipse had blinded him totally. Despite his age, his memory was sharp. He could take us to anything he had seen or heard decades back, recreating the scene with dramatic exactness. That's how he brought me to his little halt on a jungle trek.

The time was the earlier twentieth-century. The tropical plenty of South Indian forests lured many country folk into them. Villagers let their cattle graze in them while they gathered firewood or hauled hunks of valuable timber they found one way or another. Many were collecting medicinal herbs and minerals. Others checked out the hollow rocks or tree cracks for honey hives. Then there were poachers on their routine beats, and hikers and hunters out for sport. Wildlife flourished in the deeper woods, but at times it also meant deathly encounters.

My elderly friend was alone on a slope. All of a sudden, he noticed a hissing cobra with its hood up just yards away.

Those are not welcome gestures from this animal. It can squirt its venom with exact aim into a victim's eye and blind it. The cobra's fangs hold the kiss of death. However, this man wasn't frightened at all. With his left hand—-and he was left-handed—he picked up a palm-sized rock, and with a smooth force he let it fly. The rock hit the raised hood smack against a tree trunk, and the cobra went the way of all flesh.

When I got my breath back, I asked him, "What if you had missed that throw?" Most unassumingly he said that he never missed his aim in hitting anything. Never. His left hand was a precision sling.

There is some skill or gift that moves with even the least of us so that we can make sense of life and have our own bit in it. That gift—invisible though it may be—is our prime estate. We write history, our own and of the world, with it.

Story #54
Mr. Jacob and
Prime Minister Nehru

M r. Jacob had worked as a school principal in colonial times in India. He was single, and a man of ascetic self-discipline. After Independence had been won by India and after he retired, he lived many years as a lay evangelist in Delhi. He woke one morning a full hour earlier than his usual time of 5.00 a.m. and was about to set out in his schoolmasterly best, on his bicycle.

"Whereto, Mr. Jacob, this early?" asked his astonished landlord, himself an early riser.

"To see Mr. Nehru," answered the man, in his matter-of-fact tone.

That was Jawaharlal Nehru, India's first prime minister, by the way. This could not be a joke because Mr. Jacob was not of the joking kind. Older people at times take liberties with their imagination. But Jacob always was solid in word and deed.

"You have an appointment of some sort, then?" the man inquired.

"No," said Mr. Jacob, again, not much worried about the matter. Then he said that earlier in the night he had a dream in which he was instructed to meet with Nehru that very morning. In the eastern world, an ordinary man simply does not drop in on the prime minister, or for that matter, even on someone a few tiers lower, without a very good reason, and a lot of help towards it.

Well, Jacob did pedal over to Nehru's official residence, which was at least ten miles away. After parking his bike, he walked up to the security building. As they took down Mr. Jacob's personal information, they asked him what his profession was.

"I am an ambassador," said Jacob in his habitual gravity. The men saw that this would take some tactful handling, but they tried to be respectful. Mr. Jacob did not name a country of which he could be the ambassador, and it might not have helped even if he did, with his give-away native Indian looks, but you never know.

"Sir, we have a man asking to see you; he says he is an ambassador, but will say nothing more," the security office informed Nehru over the phone.

"Send him in," came the reply. A staffer from the mansion escorted him to the Prime Minister's study upstairs. Nehru invited him to be seated, but Mr. Jacob declined the honor, blaming his tight day ahead. The visitor gave Nehru a small Gideon's New Testament and said that it contained words of life that the prime minister needed. Nehru accepted the little book respectfully and asked if Jacob would sign it for him. Jacob, only minimally skilled in upward social graces, could not think of any comely phrases. He scribbled on the title page: "To Mr. Nehru, from Jacob," and then his signature. Again, Nehru received it very politely. Jacob left after a warm handshake from the prime minister.

Through the garden trail Mr. Jacob made his way back toward the guard house. As he took the bike off the stand, he looked back. Up on the terrace was Nehru standing, having been watching the man, every step on his way out. When their eyes met again, Nehru waved to Jacob, Jacob returned the wave and exited the mansion grounds.

Ten days later, Nehru died.

How did a man of no personal clout meet with the prime minister at an hour of his own choosing? He later learned that Nehru had the practice of leaving a weekly hour open for anyone who might have a reason to see the prime minister. Jacob had earlier had no idea that his visit occurred during that hour.

Story #55
Twice a Prince

A team of young people who were students of the Bible traveled to rural North Indian towns with the dean of their school. The time was well before the huge economic boom that has now changed the nation. The rural population consisted mostly of people with modest education. The visitors spoke to them about Christ and gave them some sound bites of the gospel.

In one of those towns the speaker had gone barely five minutes into his presentation of Christ, when a cry rose from the crowd: "Stop! Say no more! We know the man!" and led the team to a hut with no furniture except for a portable cot. Upon it sat a man with a flowing gray beard, glowing eyes, but in sound health, despite his age. They conversed with the man. Soon they learned that he was the heir apparent to a little princely state about a thousand miles down south. As a teenager he had heard of Christ's teachings and decided to follow him. His family was outraged by his shift of faith and kicked him out of the home. He traveled northward, crossing many state lines and settled down in this village. The villagers treated him as a vicar of heaven. The people saw no difference between him and Christ.

The student team noticed the man's little dwelling was in need of repair. In half a day they could replace its thatch and some of the rotting studs. He agreed, but when they started the work, he changed his mind and asked them not to bother. The holes in the thatch let him see the starry sky when he lay in his cot, he said. "Its beauty takes me into the pleasure of worship," he added.

Not one person returned the same after their meeting with this unknown sage. Schools and tools of learning do help us. However, a school itself can be schooled by surpassing substance.

Story #56
Udappachar: The Principal of Pre-Dawn Calls

I am glad that I met this man, and fondly wish our paths had crossed at least a decade earlier. He was the principal of a Brahmin school, well known in his day and widely respected in the city of Hyderabad in South India. The school's core faculty was made up of its alumni, Udappachar's own former students.

Mr. Udappachar knew where every student lived. Of course, that would not be difficult in places of such conservative social and domestic stability. By 5 a.m., Udappachar and four or five of his teachers would arrive, unannounced, at the home of a student randomly picked. If the kid was not at his study desk, the whole house would wake up to a knock on the front door. Once Udappachar entered the home, he would find the fellow, jog him up a bit, and let him have a slap or two. And every student knew that he had the likely but dreaded honor of a pre-dawn house call by the Principal.

Such a story will be juicy news for Western media. I can imagine the news armada tracking Udappachar's team every morning and filling the airwaves with live scenes. Well, in Udappachar's sort of world, a no-nonsense teacher like that is still revered as the guru and parent. Parents seek tough schools and teachers for their children. They seem to think that good discipline did not hurt them in their day, and so their children might also do fine.

Udappachar's college stood first in the state, throughout his tenure. For a mere 120 freshmen seats, at least 3,000 merit scholars stood in line on the only day the application forms could be purchased. The year he had hired me to teach, out of the 120 who sat for the state exams, 110 were first classes, 7 second classes and 3 third classes.

By his mid-forties, a disease called dropsy had largely disabled Mr. Udappachar. His legs and the internal organs were swollen, making all movement painful and difficult. Still, he ran the school well, the only change being the discontinuance of his pre-dawn trips to student homes.

Mr. Udappachar was awarded the presidential medal for service in education. Any number of wealthy people stood ready to help the school or Mr. Udappachar. Whenever he was hospitalized, either a donor or the hospital itself would cover all his bills.

Well-worn power is a pleasure for all under it. We owe many of our successes to people who enforced virtuous rigor on us. No sane society rejects authority worthy of reverential fear. When Prophet Samuel showed up at the future King David's village, the village elders trembled, but still welcomed him. In Udappachar's school, the fear he evoked ensured what was good in those who were entrusted to him.

Story #57
Drona and Ekalavya

Vedic India respected the teacher with reverential gravity. Even the royal court included the "Rajaguru," as the resident sage and counselor to the crown. No king would slight or second-guess the wisdom of his guru. Such was Drona, the legendary archer and trainer of the royal families of the Pandavas and the Kauravas. Among his pupils stood first the Pandava Prince Arjuna, both in merit and favor.

Out in the jungles lived Ekalavya, a tribal prince, at the mandatory remove from the mainstream castes who considered themselves vastly superior to tribespeople. Ekalavya had besought Drona as his teacher, but the haughty Drona had turned the lowly tribal away. Ekalavya would not give up. In the true spirit of a learner's reverence for the teacher, he made a clay image of Drona, and ritually installed it in the master's seat. He practiced archery within view of it, as if under the guiding eye of Drona, the Guru. His devotion seemed duly rewarded in the rapid shaping of his excellence in archery.

One day, a dog with a menacing bark strayed into Ekalavya's practice court. Ekalavya discharged an instant volley of arrows into its open mouth, still without injuring the dog, and off it ran, where else, but to the archery court of the Pandava princes. Its full mouth was proof that Drona's protégé Arjuna just might not be the top-notch archer after all. Drona himself needed to locate this unknown archer. Drona, Arjuna and the rest of the school investigated and found their way to Ekalavya's grounds.

They found Ekalavya dutifully stuck fast to his practice in front of Drona's image. The flattered guru asked the man if he had presented to his master, his *dakshana*—a ceremonial offering that marks the ritual start of one's schooling. Of course, Ekalavya had not done so because he had not been allowed to have Drona as a teacher in any formal or usual sense. Nonetheless, the woodsman was now ready to present anything possible to his master, and begged to know what might please him.

"Bring me your right thumb," the guru said. Without any hesitation, Ekalavya severed his thumb in one clean cut and set it before Drona, in a leaf. The gift was accepted. The severed thumb, Drona believed, would secure Arjuna's preeminence.

It would seem to me that a good master would heal or strengthen an organ rather than sever it to help a favorite's vanity. Consider what Christ as Master and Teacher did on the night of the Last Supper. When those disciples had a dispute among themselves as to who was the greatest among them, Jesus told them that the greatest would be the one who served the least of them. This moment was memorialized in Christ the Master washing the feet of his disciples, to model the power of humility.

Story #58
The Greatness of Quietness

I
f we consider the way of the world, Thomas Aquinas would likely have vanished into the folds of history as nothing more than a minor duke from medieval times. His father was Count of Aquino in Sicily. His mother belonged to the Hohenstaufen dynasty which ruled the Duchy of Swabia from 1079, and whose most prominent members were the German emperors Frederick I, Henry VI and Frederick II. Thomas, however, wanted to be nothing but a mendicant monk, the kind that supported themselves entirely on alms. His family disapproved of the plan and even held him under house arrest for nearly two years. Still, Thomas prevailed.

An older monk, the great Albert Magnus, famed throughout Europe, "a teacher of everything there is to know," taught and directed Aquinas. Thomas was heavy-set, slow in movement, and majestically calm. Fellow novices called him the Dumb Ox and amused themselves. Albert said to them in reproof: "This dumb ox will fill the whole earth with his bellowing." The teacher's words were prophetic.

The vocation Aquinas followed was one of saintly service in teaching and writing. In 1273, he was writing Part III of his monumental work, *Summa Theologica.* The *Summa,* which Thomas O'Meara calls "a cathedral of thought," presents thousands of questions formidably debated. While at the Mass in December of the same year, Thomas had a mystical experience in which he heard the voice of Christ. "Thomas, well hast thou written of Me; what reward wilt thou have from me for all thy labor?"

Thomas answered, "Lord, none, save Thyself."

Following this event, he quit writing for a prolonged period. Reginald of Piperno, his socius, begged him to resume his work.

At length, he said, "Reginald, I can write no more. All that I have hitherto written seems to me like mere straw."

As a commentator has said, "the great teacher of the West was silent."

Even greatness, if it grows quiet, we rate it with the weakness of the mute beast. When humility beholds or hears God, it shows why that muteness surpasses all eloquence. It will have no contest with wrangling schools.

Story #59
The Contest of Humility

As a young man, St. Benedict of Nursia came to Rome for his college education. The sixth-century Roman campus and city fully showed the repulsive excesses of the time, not unlike some places of our own times. With maturity beyond his age and wisdom beyond learning, Benedict resolved to renounce the world altogether. He fled to a cave in Subiaco, twenty-five miles southeast of Rome. Here he lived in prayer and solitude, unknown to the world. After three years, shepherds wandering the hills found him, which was enough for the start of a steady a flow of inspired followers toward him. He formed twelve monastic homes of twelve members each under a leader, himself living with a few, still separately. Among the very young sent for his tutelage were Placidus, the son of Senator Tertullus, who came "while still a child of tender years," and Maurus, the son of Equitius, a Roman noble.

As in the monastic tradition, the disciples called Benedict, "Abbot." His dwelling was home, school, and the tabernacle of worship for them, and the saint himself, more than a parent. Life was simple, and each did the needed amount of physical work besides prayer and studies. One day, Benedict sent the young Placidus to fetch water from the nearby lake. While dipping the bucket in the water, Placidus slipped and fell into the lake and was swept away from the shore by about an arrowshot. Benedict, though not at the scene, instantly saw the accident in his spirit and rushed Maurus to the lake. Placidus was still bobbing in the waves. His eyes set on Placidus, Maurus went upon the water and retrieved his brother by a hold on his hair, all the while not realizing what he had been doing. He had not jumped into the water, but had been walking on the water's surface, on the way over and back.

Back in the house, an astonished Maurus told St. Benedict of what had happened. The venerable man replied that the young disciple only witnessed the result of his own ready obedience, rather than of any merit in his master. Maurus protested that it came from no virtue of his own at all, but from the saintly abbot's command. During this contest of humility, the young Placidus had his turn to speak. He said, "When I was pulled out of the water, I thought I saw my Abbot's garments over my head and believed that he had drawn me out."

Christ says that there will be a somewhat similar exchange of personal stories at the scene of Judgment. The righteous, he says, will hear thus: "Come, you who are blessed by my Father, inherit the kingdom prepared for you from the foundation of the world. For I was hungry, and you gave me food; I was thirsty, and you gave me drink; I was a stranger, and you welcomed me; I was naked, and you clothed me; I was sick, and you visited me; I was in prison, and you came to me." Well, instead of being flattered, they are awestruck. They will ask, "Lord, when did we see you hungry and feed you, or thirsty and give you drink? And when did we see you a stranger and welcome you, or naked and clothe you? And when did we see you sick or in prison and visit you?'" Obviously, natural good will be too ingrained in them for count or recall.

Story #60
Silence, the Sire of Speech

A n obscure Jewish priest got his rare turn to serve at the Temple. While he burned incense in the holy place, the Angel Gabriel appeared to him and said, "Zacharias, your prayers are answered. You shall have a son. You shall call him John." Now, Zachariah was an elderly man, and his wife Elizabeth, also advanced in years. They were an unlikely pair now for progeny, but the news of the angel was stunningly good. The elderly priest quivered in disbelief. Gabriel would not linger nor dilly-dally with the old man's incredulity. He reminded Zacharias that he was the angel standing in the presence of God and decreed that the priest, for his doubting, would remain mute until John was born. With his errand done, Gabriel disappeared. Sure enough, when he had come out of the Temple, Zacharias had lost his power of speech. He could only use sign language.

In due course, Elizabeth, despite her age, gave birth to a male child. At his naming ceremony, a mild dispute rose. The mother said that the baby was to be named John. The people argued that the family had no such name in its past for the child to take, as was the custom. They turned to Zacharias with the question. He motioned for a plank and chalk. Upon the plank he wrote, "His name is John."

John grew up as a celibate, lived alone in the desert, matured as an adult, and appeared as a greatly revered prophet of Israel. He went about in Judea declaring that there was another One greater than he, for whom he was the herald or the "Voice in the Wilderness." Like his mother who bore him for nine months, his father too had a full nine-month term during which he would be mute and meditative. At the exact moment he was named John, the child became the anticipated voice for the Messiah, and Zacharias began to speak again. You may say, silence sired sound, both in the child and the parent.

Story #61
Two Windows

F ew kings had a prime minister of Daniel's caliber. Nebuchadnezzar brought him away from Jerusalem as a captive teen to Babylon. Himself of royal descent, Daniel was born to govern, and he excelled all his foreign peers, fully free of the lure of wealth, sex or fame. The palace found Daniel to be the crown jewel of the emperor's campaign. He served four monarchs back-to-back.

Daniel's merits did not, however, shield him from workplace politics. Cliques of disgruntled men got busy against him, possibly because of his disapproval of their ways. They hoodwinked the emperor into signing off on a new law binding all his subjects to emperor worship. Many kings in history have been touched by the "I am God" syndrome. Poor Darius also was now up for his turn.

The worship decree was the satraps' scheme to frame Daniel, whose life of personal faith was transparent. Three times a day, like any observant Jew, he would go into his upper chamber to pray. One could tell when he was in because while he prayed, he would open the window toward Jerusalem.

Daniel's chamber was at least six hundred miles northeast of Jerusalem. The Psalmist calls Jerusalem the City of God. Vast deserts lie between Persia and Jerusalem. Yet Daniel had a window that opened toward Jerusalem, his true home and the site of the Temple of God.

Could it not be said that each person is born equipped with two sets of windows: one that opens to the everyday world, and the other toward the City of God? No matter where we stand, God's city is closer to us than the zip code city under our feet. A man bound to the celestial city is the prime treasure of any empire.

Story #62
Out of the Mouth of Babes

"Guess what God told me about you, Pastor," jingled out a little girl of five or six, to a popular retreat master, who was also a priest.

"Tell me, Dear," said the pastor.

"God said that you are much too pleased with yourself, because people like you," she blurted out in one breath. The surrounding crowd stood embarrassed.

"We don't want God to say that about us, do we?" the pastor quipped back.

The little girl swayed her head in agreement. Then the priest dropped on his knees in front of the child, asking her to pray for him so that God would only see him as he should be. The little child laid her hand on the priest's head, and a spontaneous prayer followed.

Witnesses still recall the moment with brimful eyes. Humility's wisdom preached a sermon far surpassing the best examples in oratory.

Story #63
Ted Williams and the Gift of Voice

In the first week of 2011, a homeless man in Columbus, Ohio, stood at a traffic crossing with a cardboard sign of thirty-one words: "I have a God-given gift of voice. I am an ex-radio announcer who has fallen on hard times. Please, any help will be gratefully appreciated. God bless you. Happy holidays."

A reporter from *The Cleveland Dispatch* gave him a spot test and taped his sample sound bite. Overnight it went viral. Before the day ended, radio, TV and cable companies all over the nation were vying for a time slot with Ted. He was flown to New York for a large round of morning and late-night shows. Within two days, his voice sample had five million hits.

Twenty-four hours before his cyber rise to fame, Williams was panhandling for spare change. The two decades prior to that he had been living in the streets, without a street address to his name. A little plastic tent in a wayside bush was his home. Once a radio announcer, Williams had looped off into drugs, booze, and frequent brushes with the law. The best thing that happened to him was the humility to seek a second chance. America was more than ready to grant it.

The one great asset meant for his sustenance was already in him. Williams did not even have to work for it—-he and it came together into this world. He endured the needless grief of living like wind-blown debris for twenty years. Oh, what needless pain we bear!

A prophetic psalm says, "Open your mouth, I will fill it." Better yet, if you remove the vile from your mouth, it shall be like mine, says God to man. Much of our poverty or misery could be the result of either the misuse or the disuse of our mouth. As the Apostle James put it, we have not, because we ask not.

Story #64
Beowulf's Firefight

In King James's time, when neither books nor libraries were plentiful, Robert Cotton held a rare collection of Europe's major works of law, of pre-Norman English history, of literature and of manuscripts of many languages. Cotton had plenty of grateful users of his books and gained a well-deserved continental fame for it. The power of knowledge of law and government in the collection, and in the collector himself, raised enough suspicion in Charles I to order its closing as a library for a while. Nonetheless, nobles, courtiers, and even the Kings, James I and Charles II, were among the grateful borrowers of Cotton's books later on. Francis Bacon wrote his *History of Henry VII* in Cotton's library.

When his turn came, Cotton went on to the better world, and the distribution of his estate followed. His heirs found a home for his library at Ashburnham House in London. *Ash-burn-ham* lived up to its fatally ironic name when a fire swept through it in 1731, consuming its irreplaceable literary treasures. A fortunate survivor was

Beowulf, the great Old English narrative poem of over 3100 lines. The fire had, however, licked away about two thousand characters of the book's text. Possibly written in AD 700, having existed as oral narrative for two centuries prior to it, Beowulf is arguably the earliest major literary work in English.

It's frightening to think how much of what we know about our history or even about ourselves contains huge text gaps. We go "back to the future" to find the missing links of our past. It is possibly true that the modern world knows more about ancient Romans or the Babylonians than perhaps they did of themselves. What we take pride in as knowledge is at best a collection of accidental fragments that randomly came out of obscurity, be it through fire, flood, or from some caves of this earth. Yet, part-knowledge may have enough pointers to the full.

Story #65
The Screaming Sign

A young man recalled the lure of an adult showplace in a seedy part of town and how he headed toward it. He had always thought that such were the places he should steer clear of, but then he convinced himself that there was a first time for everything and that a closeted life had its own weaknesses. His heart kept thumping loudly on his way; his whole body shook and seemed on fire. He kept going, nonetheless, toward the neon signs visible from the highway. At the first turn he took toward the outfit, he saw a traffic sign which read, WRONG WAY. He froze and stood there for a good minute, but decided to complete the adventure anyway, and he did.

Years later he still could feel the firmness of what the mute sign screamed out to him, and how he still chose to go ahead. His mind, he said, could seldom rid itself of the lurid scenes that the memory of the day brought at unbidden moments. One wonders how Baalam might have felt after he had snubbed the divine admonition through the mute beast.

Story #66
Standing Low, Sitting High

C harles I of England, who you may recollect was beheaded by the Parliamentary Forces in the English Civil War, was a short man. In portraits, artists took special care not to show his majesty's want of stature. Either others could stand while he was seated, with the proportions of posture respectfully calculated, or elevation devices were set in place to enhance the regal image. Nonetheless, the lack of height did not cancel the right of state or title.

So it was with Zacchaeus, a short though rich man, about whom we learn in the New Testament. When short people themselves call one among them short, the description becomes worrisome. Anyhow, what Little Zach lacked in stature seems to have been offset by his brains. Like all others in Palestine in his day, he too desired a personal glimpse of Christ. Zacchaeus had little chance of cutting through the pressing crowd. He therefore climbed up a sycamore tree that gave him an easy vantage point.

No man has failed to see God for want of height—not of stature alone, but of social influence, racial privileges, learning, or peer ranking. Even a wayside tree is our ally in helping us to see the Man we need to see. Shade and fruit may be the only uses we assign to a tree, but its work answers also to the laws of greater worlds. Little Zach's sycamore lent him the room from where he saw the Messiah and heard his call. Coming down, he hosted the Messiah as his house guest.

Story #67
Slaves of the Great House

F rederick Douglass, the famous American slave who taught himself to read and write, and afterwards escaped from Maryland to his future greatness as a national leader of the abolitionist movement in Massachusetts and New York, gives readers a glimpse, in his autobiography, of the Lloyd Plantation in Maryland. Colonel Lloyd, the lordly owner of the plantation is shown as a shrewd and ruthless man. Douglass compares the colonel to Patriarch Job in wealth. Fifteen slaves worked in the colonel's mansion and a thousand in his fields. The mansion, its carriage house, a stable of horses of the noblest blood, and a spectacular garden drew admiring visitors from the three surrounding states.

Once a month the slaves would come to the Great House Farm of the colonel for their allowance. On the way, in both directions, they would fill the heavy woodlands with their instant songs, one after another, all in praise of the Great House Farm. No matter how they lived under the masters, the slaves would brag about the greatness of their master over others. Douglass' owner, the colonel, was often compared with a peer plantation man, Mr. Jacob Jepson. The colonel was the richest, his slaves would say; Jepson was the smartest, his slaves would counter. The colonel could buy and sell Jepson, bragged the slaves on his side; Jepson could whip Lloyd in a blink, roared the other. Usually, such exchanges ended up in skirmishes or mutual injury.

Even in misery, we have trouble letting go of our vanity. Virtue or heroism inspires the deserved song, but the need to praise the devil is a tragic mark of depravity. Moloch was pleased by the fire offering of infants. The priests of Baal, as they cried into his deaf ears did so, wounding themselves and bleeding. If my last song in life is for the Great House which only gave me great whippings, or for a god because of whose actions I yelp or bleed, must I not have missed both the right house and God himself?

Story #68
The Dare Death Diner

The fugu, known also as pufferfish, blowfish, or river pig, is to some the most alluring delicacy at home in Japan or even abroad. Japan's Shimonoseki is the "fugu city" where fishermen are known to make $100,000 in a single hour from their seasonal fugu auction. The average price of a main course of fugu is $300.

Fugu is not for the faint of heart. The fish carries a deadly toxin 1,200 times more powerful than cyanide. One milligram of it, less than the amount to fit on a pinhead, is enough to kill an adult human. A single fish has enough toxin in it to kill thirty adults. Its skin, its ovaries, and its liver hold the toxin, which take a licensed chef to separate for safety. The immediate symptoms of poisoning are muscle paralysis and numbness. There is no known antidote to fugu poison which, if ingested, can cause death within as little as 20 minutes or as long as twenty-four painful hours. Japanese law forbids serving fugu to the Emperor. Serving fugu liver is against the law, nationwide. The liver is hauled away as toxic material.

Well, in spite of all that we know about this fish, the death risk from it only enhances the fugu's appeal! Daring diners expect their skilled chef to spike the dish with a miniscule bit of the deadly liver. This gives them an instant "high," just a whiff away from fatality.

The fugu craze turns the mind to a key incident recorded in the Book of Genesis. Eden is filled with fruit of every shade, shape, and taste, but the serpent's seduction makes the forbidden fruit the prime choice for the eye. But the sure result of its taste was death, and no excuse could avert it. The fugu is the taster's choice for mere adventure, it seems, when earth's waters are teeming with fishes ranging from hook size to leviathan. We may know when and where peril could strike, but a kind of prickly pride propels us toward peril, even at the point of no return.

Story #69
Belief Beyond Belief

T he Royal house of Bikaner built the Rat Temple of Rajasthan in the early 1900s and dedicated it to Karni Mata, a devotee of Durga, the goddess of power. By a personal contract with Yama, the god of death, Karni's relatives must transition from rats to the next stage of incarnation. The temple has stood for over a century, with marble floors and gold and silver inlay in significant parts. Over twenty thousand rats have their home there; priestly caretakers and their families feed and attend to the rodent streams. Visitors come from all over the nation and beyond, many with offerings and prayers for blessing. They must enter the temple barefooted. If a rat crawls over the foot of a visitor, it means divine favor. But if the tingling foot by accident crushed a rat, reparation is due in the form of a gold or silver replacement image.

Such beliefs are scarcely in short supply. In the Suttee system of pre-modern India, a woman bereft of her husband was supposed to cast herself into his funeral pyre. The Igbos of Nigeria have a high rate of twin births, but their twins used to be thrown away into the Evil Forest because they were considered evil. In numerous cultures from the Greeks to the Chinese, the snake has been adored as a god. The more venomous it is, the larger its following.

Pascal said that the human mind is so depraved that it will believe anything that it is told – if it is told enough times. Not only is the absurd then believed, but even wars and genocide occur to preserve and elevate the absurdity. When the natural and the noble are abused, a reprobate mind may well espouse the perverse. The Creator Himself is not mocked by our choices, whatever we may think. Rather, he allows our minds to be given over to vile affections if we would rather choose those.

Story #70
Loot on Display

The British Museum and the Tower of London rank among England's top tourist draws. Their high-value displays tell startling tales of sourcing and shipping. Consider the 2,200-year-old, three-quarter-ton Rosetta Stone with the ancient inscriptions of Egypt in three languages shedding great light on the culture's past. A French soldier found it, an English officer seized it and presented to King George III, and now Egypt wants the stone back. Another Briton brought home the famed "Elgin Marbles" from the Parthenon, by permission of the Turkish governor who then controlled the area, but now Greece demands their return. Lord Byron openly called the marble looter a "vandal." The Benin Bronzes - more than a thousand (three thousand in some records) carved plaques seized through a punitive attack from the Kingdom of Benin - sailed to England and ended up being scattered through Europe. Of course, now Benin wants its plaques back. A British engineer discovered India's 1,500-year-old bronze statue of the Sultanganj Buddha in the midst of "his" project to build a railway. Birmingham metal manufacturer Samuel Thornton, on hearing of the discovery, paid £200 to have it transported to Birmingham. It is now known as the "Birmingham Buddha." The Koh-i-Noor diamond, after adorning the crowns and thrones of the Indian subcontinent for seven centuries, was plucked out of the amulet of Raja Ranjit Singh, and it is now the centerpiece of the British crown jewels.

Items collected in this manner were not a few. Tens of thousands of them from many nations are now awaiting the help of the UNESCO for retrieval or return to their homelands. Appeals for their return have seldom been successful. The reasons for denial are fascinating: The law forbids the transfer of these objects; they are the property of the state; art objects belong to the whole of humanity, not merely to one nation; these have been "given" or "sold" to the country that now holds them, and so on.

Thus, the mute icons of art do their time as glorified captives of the lust for accumulation. Bloodshed, murder and money marked the start of their journey away from their own context. Their captions say nothing of their fallen defenders. Voyeurism leads us to ogle the object, though we may marginally acknowledge the craftsman or the farsighted patron.

Story #71
The Chief's Orders

In Johannesburg, a humanitarian is killed in a botched robbery attempt at his own home. The killer is a young black man who is tricked into the act by two other youths. The man who died had dedicated himself to helping the blacks in whatever way possible. A day's journey away, his death speeds his bedridden mother's passing. The now-widowed father decides to leave his home in despair, but wants to build a dam for the village so that it may have a better future. Accordingly, he invites experts to survey the dam site and to flag the area.

Watching the flagging of the location is the Zulu village chief, a man of title, but of no power. He has no idea what these flags are for. However, he orders his own men also to pick up the flag stakes and to plant them as the others were doing. They follow the act, but the flags they plant are all in the wrong places. The experts cry out, "No, not there, not there!" The event described in Alan Paton's novel, *Cry, the Beloved Country.*

The chief's misapprehension of what is really going on and what should really be done is not unlike what many other people do. Among religious faiths, one forbids marriage to its clergy. Another lets its clergy and laity take any number of women, and the temple maids for a bonus. One forbids eating meat and even certain vegetables. Another offers meats and vegetables to the deity. Some are high-strung on times and days: they will not lend money on Tuesdays, or they will conduct weddings only on Mondays or Thursdays - and, those too, only after midmorning. Yet if you ask them why they do these things, the answer is that such is the way these things have always been done.

It is easy to amuse ourselves by the ignorance or follies of others or even to self-righteously dismiss them. What is lost in such places is the profitable occasion to examine our own flaws and to be humbled by them.

Story #72
The Shadow Show

T
he Indian state of Maharashtra is home to the big cities of Mumbai and Pune. A custom prevailed in this region forbidding entry of the so-called Untouchables, or Sudras, into its neighborhoods during the hours of the early morning after sunrise and late afternoon before sunset. Reason? The sun casts longer shadows at the start and close of the day. A Sudra who shows up at such hours for his lowly labor might cast his shadow on an upper caste Brahmin, and thus pollute him.

To be fair, Maharashtra was not alone in its repulsion at Untouchables or Sudras. In the South of India, in the state of Kerala, a Sudra on a public road had to give a hoot every minute just in case there was a Brahmin approaching from around the curve. If the two parties were within eye range, a space gap of 96 feet was mandatory. If a Sudra accidentally allowed himself to be touched by a Nair, the number two caste from the top in Kerala, that meant certain death for the Sudra, no questions ensuing. In the northern states of Gujarat and Punjab, the Sudra had to carry a broom on him to brush away his footprints from the road.

Understandably, no competition arose for Sudra jobs such as those of the barber, the tanner, the washerman, or the janitor, each of which would fetch a nickel at best for twelve-hours of manual labor every day. And if you were a Sudra woman, you earned half of what a Sudra man earned. Moreover, she must wear nothing more than a towel-width waistcloth, nothing below the knee and nothing above the waist. Of course, ornaments and footwear were out of the question.

Even the gods didn't spare Sudras, nor did the priests. The *Manusmriti* - the book which systematized the law of the Indian scriptures, the Vedas – forbade Sudras from studying the scriptures. Indeed, if a Sudra even accidentally heard the Vedas, the law enjoined that his ears be filled with molten lead and lac. If he dared to speak the words of the Vedas, he should be pulled by his tongue. If he mastered the Vedas, his body should be chopped up. You may well imagine, then, how welcome he would be if he appeared at a temple door for worship or at a university for admission to studies.

If you thought that these were social rules of the dark ages, hold on! Violence on the untouchables is a major current issue for the Indian courts. In 2010 alone, the media reported stories of Dalit women stripped naked and paraded through the streets in the states of the Punjab, Maharashtra, and Karnataka, while the police looked the other way. In 2009, a North Indian school found sixty kids dropping out overnight when the school hired a Sudra to cook the school lunch.

Human depravity comes with the devilish lust not only to rob and steal material things, and kill other human beings, but also with a devilish lust to degrade and abuse the divine dignity with which every human is endowed, whatever the caste or occupation. Rulers and systems have existed in all cultures where brutish minds in power have declared themselves gods and have required worship from their hapless subjects, especially the weaker ones. What does Satan, condemned to possess no power at all except to do evil, do when he sees the Son of God? He takes over the interview and asks for the Holy One to worship him! Instead of seeking anything redemptive, what he wants is worship of his perverse self--even a momentary bow will do. Racism and casteism are essentially similar phenomena because they are, in different cultures, the worst form of thinking ourselves superior to others for no accomplishment of our own.

Story #73
Save the Snake Pit!

T oo good to be true, and yet it is: the snake pit
is a place to favor rather than to fear. Australian
biologist Bryan G. Fry and his team can't say
enough about the good that lives in it. Industry-level
wealth resides in the mouth of the serpent, they say. And,
yes, research does show that the deadly toxin in its mouth
can be a health treasure.

Before we let our blood curdle at the phrase "snake
venom," let it be said that the venom is nothing but the
animal's protein weaponized. The venom alters a victim's
body biology, disabling the sight, nervous system, brain,
heart, or blood circulation, and shutting it all down cold.
The venom enters the target with the speed and fierceness
of a guided missile. Those who believe in evolution think
that snakes have been developing this biological weapon
over the last 80 million years!

If so, humans have shuddered at the sight of
this fearsome coiler for long enough. They now can
modify his feared fluid into great cures. What comes

out of the fangs of the copperhead inhibits cancer cell migration; the cobra delivers treatment for Parkinson's and Alzheimer's; the venom of the Malayan Pit Viper thins clogging blood; the rattlesnake helps with blood pressure medicine. Venoms of their kin are under the microscope now for potential HIV treatment.

Healing by poison is an elemental paradox. "Out of the killer comes the eat, and out of fighter flows the sweet," the mighty Samson sang in riddle. Goliath is slain with his own sword. The sting of death brings the salve of life, as science has it. The venom lives in the snake's body, as Fry himself has said, "as an evil twin" of the good protein. All evil can revert to the good it was meant to be. All it requires is a redo of its chemistry. In God's grand scheme of things, even death's hands can serve the causes of life.

Story #74
Own Nothing!

As a slave, Frederick Douglass taught himself to read and write in risky secrecy. It was illegal in the 1800's to educate a slave, or for him to learn on his own. The slave had to be on the master's estate day and night. For any outside business, he needed to carry a written permit from his owner. Without that, he could be caught for reward or even sold away for some easy felony money.

Douglass quickly applied his literacy to freeing his fellow slaves. He wrote passes for them in the name of the masters who had no idea that their slaves were capable of doing so. Douglass once led a plan for a group flight. A date and time were fixed, and all the slaves in agreement set out to the field as usual, as if for another normal working day. At a signal, each was to hit the flight trail, but only one by one, to avoid capture. As the hour approached, a sudden flash struck Douglass who said to his buddy, "We're betrayed." As they turned around, they saw overseers on horseback, seizing and whipping each slave. Douglass gave a pre-agreed signal to his men: "Own Nothing," meaning, destroy the evidence. Each man literally ate his pass.

What came out of Douglass' mouth at that "do or die moment" was inspired utterance, an ordinance of life. It comes to people at the most critical of times, at lightning speed, with the ring and rigor of a fierce command. No one reasons with it or resists it when it hits. Invariably it performs a life-changing intervention. That experience becomes indelibly memorable. Who could be the source of that command?

The slaves also had another great life lesson in that moment: Do not own, but be owned—by the author of life—which is far better than owning all of creation. Like all paradoxes in relation to spiritual realities, owning nothing and living right is not a state of penury, but the mark of infinite wealth.

One more truth: Life on earth has such an exacting design that no one, no matter who, can take anything away from this earth. Everything is held as a lease at best, and sooner or later it changes hands. The truly free are those who have happily forgone all of their mundane claims.

Story #75
A Wrestler's Lines

I n his mid-twenties, poet George Herbert stood as the Orator of Cambridge University, the public face of that entire collection of educational institutions. King James I, and King Charles I, regarded him with much respect, as did famous courtiers like Bacon, Laud, Andrewes, and Donne. Orators of Cambridge were presumed to be groomed for court positions, and so Herbert too was eyed as the future secretary of state or something similar. His brother Lord Herbert was England's ambassador to France. His mother, Magdalen of Newport, was a patron of letters.

Things worked out in an entirely different way for Herbert. Shunning the usual career ladder from that University, he became a deacon, and, eventually, a priest of the Anglican Church. A little village church in disrepair in Bemerton, near Salisbury, was his parish. He rebuilt the church at personal cost and effort. Just four years after his marriage to Lady Danvers, and just three years after his installation in the church, his tenure as curate ended with his death at the age of 39. On his deathbed, he arranged to deliver "a little book" to Nicholas Ferrar, an influential friend. That manuscript proved to be a Cambridge treasure that the world could well have lost. It contained nearly 170 poems under the title *The Temple,* which Herbert described as "a picture of the many spiritual conflicts that have past betwixt God and my soul." Craft and inspiration rarely meet in poets as they do in Herbert.

Apparently, the loss of court glory was the best turn of Herbert's life. Let's suppose Herbert had been smoothly ushered into some state office as he well deserved, and think of some of his peers who made headlines as royal favorites: Francis Nethersole, William Levett, John Ashburnham, Francis Seymour. Do we know any of them, or does anyone care? They lived and died, and we can say little more about them, but Herbert was "hurt" into poetry that voiced his agony, and speaks to us today, nearly 400 years later. An outcry emerging from a soul contending against its Creator, has a life of its own, and outweighs the worth of all earthly kingdoms put together. "All Solomon's sea of brass and the work of stone / Is not so dear to thee as one good groan," Herbert writes in "Sion," one of the poems in *The Temple.*

Story #76
Roman Emperors

G alva, Avidius, Nerva, Verus, Pertinax, Elagbalus—-ever heard of them? To save you the suspense, be it said that they were among the scores of Roman emperors who followed Julius Caesar, Augustus, and Trajan. Each of them thought that he would earn enduring fame in history, but proved scarcely worthy of a footnote. Rather than rulers, they were at best temporary fill-ins for mere days, weeks, or a few months. In the third century AD, Rome had fourteen emperors, known as "Barracks Emperors," called so because they were common soldiers who seized power by force even though they gained little by doing so. Another set, known as "Chaos Emperors" reigned over a continual state of civil war, yet not long enough even for Romans to remember their names. Gordian I reigned for 20 days, Pupenius for 99 days, both of them in the year 238. Jotapian had a few weeks in the summer of 248. Aemilianus managed just to creep into the third month of his reign, August-October of 253. And so it goes.

The title of 'Roman Emperor' undoubtedly was world's prime honor in its time, which might have been reason enough for men to want it, no matter how short the tenure. And how did they fare once they had the job? Thomas DeWitt Talmage tells us that out of the total of Rome's sixty-three emperors, only six died peacefully in their beds. In the first century alone, Rome had fifteen emperors. Of these, four were murdered, two lynched by soldiers, two committed suicide, and one was poisoned to death.

Let us not be too harsh on Rome. Read of the Arab kingdoms, of the Moghuls, of Indian rajahs or African rulers. There are differences in dates and names, sure; but the stories are essentially similar. Yet these positions never lacked aggressive takers.

And is the situation any better today? True, we don't have an Emperor anywhere in the world today. But are Presidents and Prime Ministers substantially less powerful? How about CEOs of major companies? Don't they accumulate far more wealth than most Roman Emperors ever did? Is that what explains the magnetic attraction of such positions today?

But what a price is paid for them! How quickly such positions age their incumbents! How much does stress damage their relationships, or indeed their own health?

Is that damage a price worth paying? It might be worth reflecting on the difference between chasing such a position out of your own ambition or greed, and being willing to accept such a position in order to serve because God calls you to do that. Discerning the difference between your own selfish desires and God's call, is as important to your spiritual life as it is to the destiny of your loved ones and your nation, as well as to the world as a whole.

Story #77
The Weaver's Shuttle

Weavers are like poets. A poet picks comely words out of a competing crowd, while a weaver runs the thread lines, stroke by stroke, beat by beat. Each moment moves with music and meaning. Every fabric strand tells one more bit about a great story of a war, a mythic hero, a lover's embrace, or of visionary sights.

The famed Brussels Lace is said to be spun in a dark room, with a mere beam of light shot through a small aperture, upon the forming pattern. Little by little, in intense focus, its work gets done. The finished lace is so pricey that even wealthy nations at times have restricted its import for fear of the money drain.

"My days pass swifter than a weaver's shuttle," the Patriarch Job laments in the midst of his prolonged agony. Unwittingly, he also declares the great outcome of the shuttling which is due too soon. The weaver's art, upon finishing the appointed run, will have a pattern finished and ready for display.

Some of us may have merely mild anxieties, but others may experience the terror of days fought in fear and nights full of struggles with despair. But each of us will find proven that our life's circumstances were exactly the needed setting for our full individual story, which will be on graphic display to everyone in its silliness, its foolishness, its anguish, as well as its glory.

Story #78
The Animals of Job

The Book of Job is the story of a man surprised by sorrows of epic measure, but ending in triumph. From great power and wealth, this righteous eastern sheik falls so rapidly, plundered by bandits, struck by natural disasters, all his children killed, and himself cast upon the city dump, possibly leprosy-stricken. There he sits, quarantined, scraping his scaling skin with a potsherd. Friends come to comfort, but they spend days debating why such evil befell so good a man. At last, God Himself appears on the scene, speaking to Job through a string of object lessons, two of which point to animals of extraordinary size and power.

First is the behemoth or hippo, a mammoth grass eater. His hips anchor strength, and his stomach muscles hold power; his tail is like the cedar, and his sinews are tight-knit; his bones match bars of iron; he lives in the marshes; he can take the gushing currents of the Jordan straight into his mouth.

The second is the leviathan or whale. Of comely proportions, he proudly displays his airtight scales and repels attack; his eyes gleam; his heart is flint-firm. Sword and spear are but straw or stubble to him. He knows no fear.

So, the hip to the hippo, and the neck to the whale. Do humans make the list at all? Perhaps, yes. In Psalm 8:2, King David, the lion-slayer, says, "From the lips of children and infants you have ordained strength" – strength enough to silence the foe and the avenger. The stuttering Moses delivers his enslaved nation. Elijah the mountain-loner brings rain to all of the land of the rogue King Ahab of Israel; a timid Jehoshaphat thwarts the surprise advance of a multinational army; Peter the fisherman recalls Tabitha to life; the prayer of Paul and Silas, each shackled in prison, causes a quake to open the gates and loose the shackles of all the prisoners in the city of Philippi. The applied power in each case is the strength of the suckling—the power to cry.

Story #79
Sign of Dominion

Five tons in average weight, eleven feet in height, and similar measure in length, an elephant is a little mountain of a machine. It can uproot trees or crush up a bush, knock down a boulder or get a loaded truck unstuck from mud. Yet, like a child, this calm giant serves the command of its keeper. The man signals his move to mount it, and a pillar-leg shapes itself as his ladder. The same courtesy extends as the man slides down to the ground. A scrawny little man makes this animal do what he says, even with some corporal corrections in case of slowness or hesitation.

You may think the elephant is singled out for such submission. Not really. Ancient Egyptians are said to have trained lions for help in hunting and war. Armies maintain war steeds at great expense. Canines are tamed and trained even to merit official titles and tasks. Circus groups parade bears, leopards, tigers, and other large predatory beasts as performers. Despite their great strength and even ferocity, these animals in the wild take flight when they see a human. Even the sighting of a little toddler startles most animals that inhabit the forest.

Rather than fearing peril by us, would they know how much most of us fear their power? The chance of bumping upon a lion or a hyena is an unlikely wish for a hiker. Yet, has any beast taken a human to its cage to train for his kingdom? Oh, yes, mythology has tales of wild beasts raising human foundlings to greatness, some as gods, others, at least as kings. Jonathan Swift's Gulliver discovers horses ruling over yahoos, the contemptible kind of humans. But these "animal rulers" reign in books only.

Speaking of books, the Book of Genesis privileges humans with dominion over all creation, in the sense of caretaking. Nature columnist Larry Lyons of *The Niles Star* thinks that animals themselves might have been telling their offspring of some point in human history where something entered life that brought fear and its cause with it. That should explain, Lyons adds, why a 1,500-pound moose bolts for cover when it sees a human one-tenth of his weight. After all, animals did come voluntarily and without fear to Adam. Adam named them correctly, meaning, he named them with the accurate understanding of their nature. Adam's call must have been in the dominion of love. Likewise, they entered Noah's ark with no sign of fear. If the nature of Nature itself changed with Adam's fall because of the entry of the principle of death into the world, isn't it interesting that, in the Biblical record, the nature of Nature changes once again with the Flood, so that animals become instinctively afraid of humans? Of course, we are instinctively afraid of most animals too, whether big ones or small ones such as snakes, mice, and even spiders. However, we can and do learn to overcome our fear of animals in order to govern them or look after them (though we too often merely exploit them or, worse, abuse them). Is there a parallel somewhere there of our need to overcome also the "inner beasts" that too often drive us?

Story #80
Fear, the Goldmine

A new professor in his late twenties was hard at work, day and night, getting the manuscript for one of his books ready. It seemed as though he was racing to the finish line of his life, despite the promising start.

"You are a great model of industry, Pietro," I commented.

"No, it's called fear," he quipped back.

Why should a successful, young man like him fear? Well, if he fails to establish himself as a scholar, big regrets might beset him.

Fear is a good driver. In fact, we need fear to keep life going. It is the fear of hunger that gets us to work. Bankers know that they do well when fear of want drives people to save. Nations build their defenses for fear of their enemies. Fear tempers all buying and selling. Buy a home; sooner rather than later, buy insurance for it, against fire, flood, or break in. Buy a car, but buy also the extended warranty, and buy insurance to cover accidents. A cargo ship or oil tanker is on the dock, but release it only with escort and insurance against perils on the sea and piracy. Each time you set out to do something, there arises an implied bet of fear. It is a bet you can't win.

Fear reigns even where pleasure dwells. A dancer's foot, a singer's voice, a model's smile, a harvest yield, a cruise ship, or the greatest museums – all these yield well to fear. Without fear, most of the world would have been dirt poor. Fear takes life hostage, but it also pays out rewards for the experience, unwelcome though it might be.

Story #81
The Twin Sense

Two adult twins living on the two sides of the Atlantic, always reportedly knew when the other suffered pain. A call to check out the pain event would prove each man right every time. Then one of them was all of a sudden taken by a serious illness with physical suffering. The other twin was immediately in the grip of intense anxiety for three full hours, the end of which coincided with his dying brother's last breath. In a similar instance, a sister visited her twin, and while saying goodbye, the other felt that it might be their last meeting. From that moment on, she began to shake restlessly, fearing some impending evil. News came next morning that the visiting twin of the night before had been killed in a pre-dawn automobile accident.

The well-known twins St. Benedict and St. Scholastica, siblings of a 6th-century Roman family, both chose monastic living, devoting themselves fully to prayer and service. The two would meet on an annual visit at a mutually convenient midpoint and return to their monastic homes before the mandatory curfew hour.

At their final meeting, Scholastica urged her venerable brother to converse a little longer, but the rule-abiding Benedict insisted that he must be back on time at the monastery, even though he himself was the head of the order. Without pressing her brother further, Scholastica dropped her head on the table for a moment's silent prayer. A heavy thunderstorm came down over the place where all was clear a minute ago. Benedict had no choice but to stay there until the rains cleared after several hours. Three days later, in a vision Benedict saw the spirit of his sister enter the clouds of glory in the form of a dove. That very moment he announced that his sister had entered eternity.

So too, when the young Thomas Aquinas died in Italy, his elderly master, Albert the Great, in Germany knew it instantly. Albert broke down sobbing, saying, "Thomas Aquinas, my son in Christ" is dead. He was right.

It may be that we are all privileged with strengths of which we are either unaware or unmindful. Life *in* this body holds more than the life *of* the body. Many forms of knowledge are at work in us. In the ideal world, our power to sense pain is not confined within the confines of our body alone but extends to all on earth. If we can sense others' pain, is it possible that we have the means in us to do something about it as well?

Story #82
The Rod of Levi

M oses and his older brother Aaron, both in their eighties, were the men chosen to lead Israel in their forty-year journey through the desert of Sinai. This was a job that Moses never sought but was thrust upon him. None could do what Moses was made to do -,unless God did every part of it. Try making a plague come and go, or parting the ocean with the waving of a rod, or striking a rock to produce a gushing stream out of it, and you will know what the job involved. If your success in a job depended wholly on what came from a source that you could not control, what would be the point in taking it over by art or force?

Yet, men challenged Moses. Three men—Korah, Dathan,, and Abiram—conspired against him and created a powerful political following. They appeared in their priestly vestments and with their fire-filled censers for a united show of power. Perhaps the move was designed as a ceremonial coup d'état. A mysterious fire immediately consumed those men and 250 of their followers, even as they were making their offering. An earthquake at the same hour devoured their dwellings with their wives and children. Nonetheless, the uprising only got stronger. That's where the rods appear.

At God's command, Moses took the twelve rods, one from each of the twelve tribes of Israel, with each leader's name inscribed on it. The rods lay before the ark of God for a night. The next morning Moses retrieved them for return to their owners. Every one of them got his plain stick back, except Aaron. Aaron's rod differed from those belonging to all of the rest. Overnight, in the Holy of Holies, it budded, blossomed, and bore almonds. The still stick, that might be considered as good as dead, under the eye of God, in the silence of the night, stirred with new life.

While the lusting leaders fought for undeserved titles, divine life overruled all rival claims. A night in the right place sets up the soul for an unfading day.

Story #83
The Unblessable

I am close friends with a community leader in a big city. This man is the arch-parent of his people there. In his tastes and training he is of the older school, but he moves with the young and old alike. Most of the youth think well of him and give him the respect due.

Not so, however, is one of the young men in his circle that I also knew. He has an evident air of sneering superiority toward most people, this leader himself not exempt. The young man has looks, wits, and wealth. But his disdain for others makes him tough company. He is politically smart enough to say nothing wrong within the hearing of others, but his body language does the work, instead.

My friend the community leader keeps his hurts to himself, and believe me, he has no lack of them. The proverbial extra mile is his personal standard. In a late-night phone call, he told me that he had invited the arrogant young man for lunch the next day. The intention of the meeting was for this private time to help create some measure of warmth in the cocky youth, but he wanted me to pray with him because he knew the task would not be easy. "So gifted, but so unblessable," said my friend warily of the young fellow. There was such heartbreak in that one word "unblessable". We prayed that that would not become a life sentence.

We may not be publicly cocky, like that young man, but the anecdote raises the question: what areas of our lives do you and I keep "unblessable"?

Story #84
Signed and Sealed

American Poet Sylvia Plath came up in a recent campus conversation. Plath was married to British poet Ted Hughes, from whom she had been separated after the birth of their second child. On a February morning in 1963, this bright woman stuck her head in the oven and gassed herself to death, while her two little children under the age of three were still sleeping in the nearby room. Breakfast was set on the table for them.

"I wondered why such a promising life had to be thus undone," I said as an open comment.

"Intellectuals do not reconcile with life easily," said a colleague.

"That explains why most of us are still alive," responded another.

Well, this is not to make light of human misery or personal tragedies. Plath is not alone in this kind of date with destiny. Anne Sexton, her contemporary who consistently wrote about depression, sexuality, and death, also ended her life by toxic gas. Poet Denise Levertov described Sexton's suicide as "creativity in death rather than self-destruction." Sarah Kofman, a Sorbonne philosopher, and author of several works on Freud and Nietzsche, killed herself on the 150th birthday of Nietzsche. According to philosopher Jack Derrida, this was her way of giving to Freud and Nietzsche a return of the "inheritance she had received of them." Virginia Woolf, a modern literary voice, chose to drown herself in the river Ouse in Sussex, weighing her coat pockets with stones. Add to these the names of Hart Crane, Ernest Hemingway, John Berryman, F. O. Matthiessen, or scores more from a recent count of over seventy writer-suicides.

Michael Foucault, the French philosopher who died after a series of suicide attempts and finally of AIDS in 1984, wrote and spoke of suicide as "the simplest of pleasures" at one's disposal. If he had a billion francs, he said, he would create a service of "retreats" for suicide preparation, "suicide festivals and suicide orgies," with every desired pleasure accompanying, including drugs.

Admirers praise these dead for "walking their talk," through deaths that matched their scripts. What is widely overlooked is the utter absence or the defiant rejection of spiritual truths in their lives and works. Great poets are not so; Philip Sidney in *The Defense of Poesy* notes that poets are *vates,* meaning, seers or prophets, who receive "the highest knowledge hidden to the world." With that gift, they "show the way, entice any man to enter it," says Sidney, "winning of the mind from wickedness." The *vates* deliver us the word that we can use, live by, or even help us transcend ourselves. Ethan the Ezrahite, Solomon, Valmiki, Homer, Dante, or Tagore sing of the triumphs possible even in a torn world, unlike those who only record the sounds of their choking gasps or the rip of life's very fabric.

Story #85
A Senseless Price Tag

R ussell Conwell, the founder of Temple University, was a popular speaker whose charm of common sense was his selling strength. He delivered a single speech entitled "Acres of Diamonds" over five thousand times all over the nation, and still had no trouble finding new audiences.

Conwell speaks of a Pennsylvanian farmer who would do what any Penn farmer would do in those days: he sold it, but not until he had his new job firm. He had a cousin in Canada in the coal oil business. He wrote to him for a job. The Canadian turned him down the request because the American cousin knew little about coal oil. Not to be slighted that way, he began to read up on everything there was to know about coal, "from the second day of creation clear down to the present time," and convinced his cousin to hire him, which he did. The American sold his Pennsylvania farm for "$833 and no cents" and headed up to Canada.

Twenty-three years later, the man who bought his property noticed a huge buildup of scum over the farm creek. Tests followed. The state geologists confirmed the presence of a vast bed of coal oil in the dammed-up area, worth a hundred million dollars in taxes alone to the state—- all on the property that was sold for $833 and "no sense" by someone who had read so much about the subject.

There are people who are foolish because they are ignorant. And then there are people who are foolish because they don't apply what they know. You and I may pride ourselves on not being the first kind of fool. But in what areas of our lives are we in danger of being the "knowledgeable fool"?

Story #86
The School of Child Mothers

The Frayser Middle school of Memphis, Tennessee, made headlines in January 2011 because of 90 pregnant teenagers, none older than sixteen. Twenty percent of Frayser's students are already parents. That number is predicted to move upward as the pregnancy timeline advances for the rest. Frayser must provide instruction, along with prenatal and childcare for its pupils, as do schools across the nation. The June 2008 *Time* story takes us to Gloucester, Massachusetts, where the daily line up for pregnancy tests is part of the school clinic's work. Seventeen girls of Gloucester had a successful "Pregnancy Pact" where they would all be mothers in a single cohort. The pact pattern, though not announced, was true even of Frayser, according to NBC.

The students were expecting "high fives" and baby showers, and some kind of status-elevation through the adventure of early motherhood. The child-mothers come to school, to the convenience of childcare provided on campus. The schools are expanding facilities and services, "in-school and after-school," with additional funding. According to one expert, young girls explore sex for the sake of love and acceptance; she also faulted the county for not having an OBGYN in the school area of Memphis to help the girls. The Massachusetts school didn't have that problem. In fact, the Gloucester school doctor and the nurse would prescribe contraception pills to any student, regardless of parental consent. Many of the girls were only upset if they were not yet with child.

While in her position as First Lady, Hillary Clinton popularized the African proverb, "It takes a village to raise a child." That village in Africa, however, lives by its proven values whereby a child is allowed to grow first. From a camp different from Clinton's, General Colin Powell said that children ought to be taught safe sex practices—in the elementary school, that is, by the way.

A man from the famous Judean village said, "May our sons be like goodly plants and our daughters like pillars carved to adorn a palace." This villager was King David, of whom daughters of Israel famously sang, "Saul killed his thousands, but David his ten thousands." His son Solomon was a king and a poet. Solomon's hero in the Song of Songs declares this of his love, a chosen daughter: "You

are a garden locked, a spring enclosed, a fountain sealed."
Does anyone sing today about America's daughters as the
sealed fountains of the enclosed gardens? And does all that
State provision at taxpayers' expense lead to fulfilled lives
for these teenage mothers – or their children?

Story #87
Philoctetes' Wound

I f Greek mythology tells you a story, you can be certain that the very same story is told in a variety of alternate forms, with new twists in each. One such is the legend of Philoctetes, a Greek war hero, a suitor of Helen of Troy. He was the armor bearer of Heracles from whom he inherited a celebrated bow and unerring, poisoned arrows. On the way to Troy, he entered the temple of Athena in Chryse, unfortunately getting too close to the temple serpent that bit him. The venomous bite resulted in an ulcerated wound of intolerable stench. Odysseus, the King of Ithaca, ordered that he be left behind on the island. Ten years later an oracle ordered him brought into the Greek ranks for the war to end successfully. As he rejoined the Greek ranks, Apollo arranged for his healing through another complex story.

Literary critic Edmund Wilson made an interpretive point out of Philoctetes' condition as a stranded and disabled man. This man is skilled in archery. He is divinely gifted with unerring accuracy. Loneliness and pain are his enduring companions. In spite of the pain, or even because of the pain, his aim is always accurate. So is the case with the artist, whose creative solitude and inner agony help in producing works of art with severe exactness and wholeness of effect. At least that is what is argued by Wilson.

Whether or not you buy that argument, there is no question about the value of pain. A person who has not been tested by trials cannot become a good leader. Grief is a great formative force. When we are purged of our superfluities, we speak with gravity and without pretense. That's why the tragic heroes of Sophocles, Shakespeare, or Marlowe are so memorable.

At the climax of his suffering, the hero Job, in the Old Testament cries out, "O, that my words were graven with an iron pen and lead, in the rock forever!" Moses became so richly usable once he acquainted himself with the afflictions of his people. Israel's great King and bard, David, sings in praise of his affliction, the very thing his useless grandson Rehoboam lacked, and thus ruined the legacy.

When you are wounded, take your woundedness to God. In His love, he only allows suffering to come to you in order to prepare you for moral and spiritual greatness. Whether we take that opportunity from God, or rebuff it to retreat into our own hell-hole, is entirely our choice.

Story #88
Poverty in Mansions

About fifty people gathered for a reception for Dr. K.N. Nambudripad in a large suburban home in the American Midwest. A man of radical simplicity, Nambudripad was a brilliant neurosurgeon, a professor of medicine, and the head of Christian Medical College of Ludhiana in India. His knowledge had a pleasant blend of classical Indian learning and European hands-on skill. Often, he spoke on matters of faith with disarming depth and authority.

Well, Dr. Nambudripad stood up to speak. In the middle of his talk, he made an innocent observation about the many houses that he had visited. The houses were built at great cost. No amenity or charming convenience was spared. Yet, most of them lacked one thing: there were no books at all. The needs of the mere body are lavishly met by the store and supplies in the house, but will not the mind of the resident starve to death?

Does the absence of good books betray a home as a mental wasteland? Not only do some places not have books, but they also adamantly stay that way. Thomas Fuller b̥emoans the destruction of books by decree or disaster as "massacre of monumental intellects." In the Danish invasion of England, and Henry VIII's takeover of monastic properties, the highest casualties as we look back, was the destruction of some (i.e., Roman Catholic) books in the libraries where each book came out of the labor-intensive, manual copying by monks. The same could be said of Mongol burning of the House of Wisdom in Baghdad, or Bakhtiar Khilji's alleged torching of Nalanda's library.

A good book, says Milton, is the precious life blood of a master spirit. The value in a book is beyond the reach of money. If so, a home is impoverished by not having it, and so is a person. Apostle Paul instructs his protégé Timothy to bring along his cloak and his books which he left at Carpus' home. Whenever Timothy is able to sail back from Troas, down the Aegean Sea into the Mediterranean Sea, past Crete and then past Sicily, and finally up the Tyrrhenian Sea, all the way to Rome – a long journey! – of all things in the world, the only things that Paul wants him to bring along are just his cloak and his books.

Story #89
The Teacher's Wink

A conference speaker in Delhi was talking about people who talk faith, but do not bother "doing" it. Even people who make a living in the name of faith often stay clear of its practical end. To drive home the point, he recalled his own grade schoolteacher, a good man, who had an involuntary habit of a continual wink. His speech and his wink didn't sync. In fact, the wink often worked against his word. He would tell his pupils, for instance, that the earth is a planet spinning on its axis and orbiting the sun, and as soon as he finished the statement, he would wink as if to say, "Naah, just kidding!"

That reminded me of the Pharisees and the Sadducees of Jesus' days. These two religious parties differ in their beliefs though they both belong to the same faith. As the more conservative branch of Judaism, the Pharisees go over the edge with their fussy "do's and don'ts." Keen on tithing, even on tithing cumin and bay leaves, and carefully observant of all rituals, they strain out the gnat but swallow the camel, as Jesus put it.

A contemporary illustration of Pharisaic type of influence might be the following: tourist reports mention two kinds of elevators in some Israeli hotels—one that takes the rider straight to the selected floor, and the other that stops at every floor so that the Orthodox rider would not exceed the permissible distance limit of a Sabbath's journey.

Of course, Pharisees also reject the Rabbi who taught that the Sabbath was meant for man rather than man for the Sabbath.

As for the Sadducees, their story is even better. They stood on the opposite extreme, constituting the priestly and political elite of Israel in Jesus' time. They did not believe in angels, resurrection, afterlife, visions, or mystical experiences which most world religions claim as part of their teachings. The Sadducees had little trouble running the temple, its massive finances, and its "religious work" (the ceremonies and rituals) while they appear to have had little faith in what the temple itself stood for!

The same holds true of interpretations of diverse faith streams today. Supernatural events occur throughout the Bible, and experts enjoy the airtime to talk about them even though they have little experience of them in their own lives. "They were true long ago, but have ceased to be," is their settled drone. Others argue that miracles were all figurative – little more than a trick by which a gripping tale is told.

Are not such theorists bested by history's witnesses? The Jansenists of the seventeenth-century affirmed the miraculous with flowing proofs of signs and wonders among them, but the Jesuits who belonged to the same faith at the same time would have none of it. The Desert Fathers of Egypt, Francis of Assisi, Joan of Arc in medieval France, Savonarola in Renaissance Italy, and the leaders of various holiness revivals of recent times often lived in the supernatural as if it were their natural. A large evangelical block appears text-happy with the good book, but they too have experts and schools who say, "Well, maybe long ago, but not now."

It appears that the teacher's wink keeps flashing through every era.

Story #90
An Epic Contract

J ohn Milton, the English poet of unequaled learning,
set goals for his life that were stately. Traveling as
a younger scholar in continental Europe, he had
made known to John Mansus of Naples his desire to write
a major poem, something of the scope of the Arthurian
legend. Three decades later he offered the world the great
epic, *Paradise Lost,* vastly greater than any other work in
the British world.

And what would Milton earn from this opus of a
lifetime?   On April 27, 1667, Milton contracted with
publisher Samuel Simmons of London for the first edition
of *Paradise Lost* with an advance of £5.00. Another £15
would follow in three installments if three editions sold
1300 copies each or more. They did, but Milton lived long
enough to receive only £5 more. Lest you be disheartened,
Milton's widow received another £8 in the year of Milton's
death. To save you the pain of the math, be it said that the
great bard's work fetched him an astounding total of £18,
split over at least a two-year period!   If his life depended

on this kind of income alone, I am not sure if Milton would have returned to his writing desk.

There is no telling how many scores of editions of Milton's works have appeared since. It would be a big actuarial project to determine how many millions have read them and how much revenue the works have generated for their publishers and will continue to do so, not a penny out of it going to Milton.

Supreme labors are too great for price tags or trade. Caxton's printing press, the Wright brothers' flight experiments, vaccines for tuberculosis or polio, or heroic leaderships in national movements—-who could pay enough for any of them? Who could assess and compensate Moses for his life and work as poet, prophet, healer, liberator, lawgiver, and the very type of the Messiah King? He sets a nation free from four centuries of slavery, moves them across the sea and the desert, works and moves under miracles, and leads them to the edge of the Promised Land, yet dies without entering it. He does nothing to make himself or his children prominent. Yet the name of Moses is central to the life of Israel, and his work has pervasive influence on the whole world.

Priceless labor is unrewarded, partly because it cannot be. The labor itself is its reward.

Story #91
The Messiah among the Monks

A small monastery had been existing like an old dry tree in a desert. About fifteen monks lived there, the youngest among them in his early eighties. It had not attracted a single new member for decades. The abbot of the house was saddened that once he had passed on, the house would also cease to be.

The abbot decided to visit another monastic house at about day's journey away. This most likely would be his last visit to his fellow monks at this location. They received him warmly, and as monks do, they spent their time together mostly in prayer and reflective conversation. Little else happened. The abbot had to return the next day. As he prepared to depart, his host said, "Oh, by the way, I forgot to say something to you last night." The visitor stood expectantly. The host went on: "While in prayer, I learned that one among the sixteen members of your house is the Messiah."

When he returned home, all the abbot's monks gathered around to greet him. "Was there a word from our brethren of the other house, Father?" they queried.

"No, they told me not much of anything at all. My visit time was spent in quiet reflection. However, as I was about to leave, the Abba said that one of us in this house is the Messiah."

What they heard lifted their spirits. Rather than trying to single out the Messiah from among them, each began to see traits of the Messiah in the other as they conversed and moved about. Their mutual encounters became Messiah moments. Before long, the monastery began to draw streams of visitors who also discovered marks of the Messiah in one and all. With the support of their donations, the desert began to blossom. The monastery of the wilderness turned again into the oasis that it once was, full of clustering blossoms.

Have you perhaps found your life changed for good or ill by a single sentence or word by someone? Many people have. Is it worth considering well each sentence, each word, that is expressed by you, whether vocally, digitally, or by any other means?

Story #92
The Desert Snake

I recall a journal describing the creativity of a desert snake. It finds a spot—just about anywhere might do, I should think—and it coils itself into a perfect cylinder about one foot high, gleaming fully in the sun. Now it looks like a steel drum, brimful with water, with shades of movement in it as a bird flying overhead notices it. It must be a little oasis or a vessel of some sort with water up to its edge, thinks the bird – and lands on the "rim" of the round, shiny vessel for a welcome drink. In an instant, the vessel disbands with a whistling whip, the bird's neck already in its mouth. There is no escape.

I suppose I don't have to go to the Arab sands or the Sahara to see this game of death thus played out. It happens every day where the gullible are taken in the snare of the crafty. Temptation follows everyone, and the power to repel it takes resolve even before it shows itself. No snare comes except with shining face, but it leads only to the vaults of Hades.

Story #93
The Seed in Vigil

L
ate in the 19th century, Professor W. J. Beal buried twenty sealed bottles of seeds for periodical planting after every ten years. That means the seeds would be brought out of their dormant storage for open planting after decades of no exposure at all to the open world. For 120 years now, the rotating batches of those seeds have been germinating from this source stock. Five more bottles remain in slumber, says the status report. The last one is set for 2050. Botanists at Michigan State University where the bottles rest are confident that the seeds will continue to be viable.

It is already known from tests in other places that seeds can keep themselves ready for the future well beyond a hundred years, two hundred, or even more. The lotus seed, found in various parts of the world, can stay dormant for 2,000-3,000 years, and when it wakes up, it is good to go.

Like a perpetually watchful intelligence operative, the seed preserves itself within its own fortress, and responds when rightly placed in the soil. According to botanist D.

B. Desai, as little as 1/1000 of a second's contact with a glimmer of light may suffice for certain seeds to break open in warm, moist soil.

Plato tells us the allegorical tale of a cave where captive men sit bound in darkness. They, however, see shadows of passing figures outside of the cave reflected on the cave wall, but never witness the light itself that brings about the shadows. And then one of them goes out to experience the light for the first time ever; he returns to tell his peers of the beauty of the light, to find himself only rousing their suspicion and antagonism.

The seed says it better than Plato does, and it has been doing so much earlier than Plato ever could. Every human is a candidate for the spark of light from the Creator, which will set him or her free of captivity, at a divine moment. The little seed that declares it through its own life is as much the apostle of light as any other, for God can make a blade of grass his text, a sparrow his herald, or the little bee his knight.

Story #94
The Value of Clean Hands

T he time is 1847. Ignaz Semmelweis, a Hungarian professor of medicine, is much troubled that up to thirty percent of women die of childbirth infection at the Vienna General Hospital.

Semmelweis had a strong hunch that the deaths in the birth ward were due to the lack of cleanliness. Surgeons and medical students were moving from autopsies to deliveries with unwashed hands. The infective particles stuck around the fingernails of a treating physician would be enough to kill a surgical patient. To test out what he suspected, Semmelweis required chlorine washing of hands and surgical instruments before and after each treatment. Immediate differences registered. The high, double-digit death rates dropped to less than one percent. Later statistics confirmed his claims further.

Instead of crediting the surgeon for any good, Semmelweis's colleagues held him up to ridicule and scorn for his cleanliness theory. Some felt insulted that Semmelweis would suggest that they wash their hands. He was bypassed in promotions, despite his credentials.

He wrote to doctors all over Europe that the thousands of needless deaths by infection could be averted by a simple step of washing that cost them nothing.

Semmelweis still received only mocking responses, which enraged him, provoking abnormal behavior. His family and the dwindling circle of friends concluded that he was insane. Even his wife concurred, and Semmelweis was committed to an asylum. There the man died within two weeks, ironically, of the same infection in his body caused by physical injuries from the guards.

The germ theory of Louis Pasteur eventually proved Semmelweis right. Within a decade of his death, Joseph Lister followed upon Pasteur's work and introduced principles of antiseptic treatment which fully defended Semmelweis' honor, though he had died unrewarded.

Back to the hands once more. Hands are figurative of all that we do. They have the power to comfort, to crush, to save, or even to slay, as the user chooses. Think of that unforgettable scene where Macbeth, after killing the innocent King Duncan, cries out in horror, seeing in his hands the horror of his deed:

> Will all great Neptune's ocean wash this blood
> Clean from my hand? No; this hand will rather
> The multitudinous seas incarnadine,
> Making the green one red.

> (Macbeth II.ii. 57-60)

Macbeth at least feels guilt. Some there are who murder and feel no guilt. However, the power to kill lies in each of our hands. Sometimes the killing can be unintentional – for example, when a caregiver might be carrying an infection without being aware of it. In such a case, to know that a caregiver's infected hands have the power to kill is the first step towards a person's protection. Soap may clean the hands of obvious uncleanness, and lye may purge the fingertips of putrid matter, but the soul needs the washing by the waters that lead to the altar of God. Could we learn more about such things if we meditated more on the Apostles being commissioned to lay hands on the sick for their healing?

Story #95
A Law to Flee

A Bangladesh mullah issued a fatwah that a fourteen-year-old rape victim should receive 101 lashes for her alleged relationship with a married man. The man was her own older sister's husband back home after a season of employment as an expatriate worker in a more prosperous country. Ever since his return, the girl's father and sister noticed that the man had been eyeing the girl. It wasn't too long before he caught the girl on her way to the outdoor latrine, dragged her to the nearby shrubbery, gagged and raped her. Hearing the muffled cry of the girl, her older sister, the rapist's wife, ran to the scene, dragged her back into the house, beat her and kicked her.

The village elders took the news to the Imam who ruled 101 lashings for the girl and 201 lashings for the man for "adultery." The punishment was to be public in Shariatpur, near Dhaka.

The lashings were set to go, for the man first, but he escaped. Then they turned to the girl. She took seventy lashings, and then collapsed to the ground. She was taken to the hospital where she died a week later. The autopsy said that Hena Begum's death was by suicide. The government reports that even though fatwah punishments are illegal, Bangladesh sees an average of 500 such judgments carried out every year.

Go back to the gospel times for another adultery trial. John 8 shows the effort of a religious mob seeking the life of a woman who has just been "caught in the very act," and thrust in front of Jesus for his verdict. Her accusers cite Moses' Law against such conduct. Jesus appears unperturbed, and without even looking up, he keeps scrawling in the sand, with apparently little regard for their morality policing.

The mob demands his "fatwah" on the woman. Instead of the whip of the lictor, each man has a rock in hand, ready to hurl. No sooner had they finished speaking, than Jesus gives the verdict: "He that is sinless among you, cast the first stone." One by one the stones drop, and the men trickle away, starting with the oldest. "Has none of your accusers condemned you?" Christ asks the woman. "No, Master," she answers. "Nor do I," says he, and lets her go, telling her to keep herself pure henceforth.

Evidently both the law and the judge failed the Dhaka victim of sexual violence. The felon is enjoying his shadowy safety somewhere. The mullah and his court are satisfied that they did their duty according to their established practice. The letter of the law killed defenseless victim of unchallenged brutishness.

Good law embodies love. Love is its soul. Apart from love, law only can spell death. Good law is redemptive, holding out the moral and material means for the wellbeing of individuals and nations. When implemented, such love turns humans into angels and brings heaven down to this earth.

Story #96
The Unspared Strength

L ong ago my older son asked of me a childhood memory for a school report of his. The face of a schoolmate of my own early days quickly came to my mind. His name was Goldie. I knew him, though not closely. The whole school knew him the same way, mostly as a victim of cruel mockery. Goldie had scars of severe burns all over his body, but I never asked him how those thick burn scars came about. His face was larger than normal, the neck veins and skin all stuck together and taut. He had to turn his whole body around to look sideways or backward. He dragged one leg along as he walked. Goldie's speech was a labored lisp, possibly from some damage to his vocal cords. He was an easy target for bullies, and even for the cowardly.

About a quarter mile north of the school stood a church facing the road. A little shrine stood at the church entrance, like a little toddler in tow with the mother. Wayfarers would pause at the shrine to light a candle or to drop a coin in its offering chest. Right after school, the church road had flowing crowds of kids, all heading toward the four-way junction further up.

On my way back from school one afternoon, I heard a loud cry from around the church shrine. As I looked up, who do I see but Goldie, standing right in front of the shrine, with his head skyward and wailing out to God! His books lay scattered on the ground. Some kid had assaulted him on the road, just for the vain thrill of it. Of course, Goldie could not defend himself, and it mattered to none. He limped the few paces into the church grounds and brought his cry to the only person he imagined might care. I do not know how long he stood there or what he did afterwards. I walked on, as did the many scores of his peers, letting him fend for himself.

I walked on: that is a sentence I still hold against myself. I think of that moment only with sheer shame. Why did I walk away from a child like me whom I saw so meanly wronged? Why did I not walk *toward* him, instead? Even as a frail eleven year old, I possessed some strength, however little it was. I did not have to be a giant to stand by him. I could at least have shown him that he was not alone. The fact is that though I was not insensitive, I was far too shy and nervous to court notice at such an emotional scene. I lacked the good sense to know what to do. It would have cost me nothing to walk up to give him a hug, and to walk him home at least partway, and it would have meant more than all the world to him.

I was his sufficient strength that failed to serve when no other person filled the void.

This was an elective tragedy, a needless denial of a comfort I withheld.

Story #97
The Trickle's Push

A handful of us were giggling like little kids while wading in the shallow headwaters of the Mississippi. Here was a little burbling stream in the Northern Minnesota town of Itasca, tickling at our ankles. A drop of rainwater falling here would be in the Gulf of Mexico, ninety days and 2,550 miles later, but not before the stream has swollen in size and strength with her numerous sisters and matrons, who would join her along the way. Their confluence would shift swelling river into roaring rapids and mighty breadths. What barely rose to my knee at its start, is 200 feet deep in Louisiana, where it takes a bridge 24 miles long to cross it. As the river goes, so it grows.

Okay, let us see how the great Amazon fares in comparison. The river had been in business probably for millennia but, at least for the last many centuries none could tell where the riverhead was. After four decades of modern search, the National Geographic explorers pinpointed the origin of the Amazon to "a trickle of water coming off a cliff high in the Peruvian Andes," - more precisely, in the Carhuasanta Stream in Nevado Mismi in Southern Peru! That "trickle" starts what becomes, with more than a thousand tributaries, the sure spread of a water basin covering seven South American nations. The result? Even in the dry season the river has widths of seven miles, and triple that in the flood months. The depths of the river are good enough for ocean-sailing ships to come two-thirds of the length up the river. The Amazon's mouth that cuts its entry into the Atlantic is 202 miles wide, some say 250, with such power in its thrust that it pushes the Atlantic's salty waters 100 miles back into the ocean, thus keeping the whole sea area still fresh.

The trickles of any river tell the perennial human story. A single human is on a journey like the lone trickle at the river's start, yet within that human may be powers that far exceed our likely need. Bound with those around us in oneness, our story becomes massive. When unlearned and ordinary folk came together in one accord on and after the day of Pentecost, the earth shook, prison gates broke, and tyrants fell. Those who had been timid became valiant, besieged the Kingdom of Heaven, and became channels capable of changing their world. Each lone drop pushed back the salty sea and changed its taste then, and it still does.

Story #98
The Idea of the Image

I n the early years of the 21st century, Dr. Robert Smith, a surgeon at Scotland's Falkirk Royal Infirmary, became the hot target of a media hunt. He had amputated the legs of two perfectly healthy young men. These "private patients" just felt that legs were unnecessary and wanted their bodies to be rid of them. Dr. Smith's team complied with the demand at £3000 each for the surgery.

Experts argued that these young men had a psychological illness known as Body Dysmorphic Disorder. Such persons just do not like their looks and are obsessed with the desire to change into a shape that their brains dictate. The brain has a "map" of the body, which gives the patient a supposed image of it. If the supposed and the real shapes differ, in the old days one could only *reimagine* the body; today, one has the actual possibility of *reimaging* it. Some become suicidal with their felt need for change. If amputation requests are declined, they frame accidents or injuries that make the removal of their disliked organs unavoidable. On the milder side, some pretend being maimed, or wear artificial limbs over the healthy ones as a "remedy" to their claimed disability.

I wonder if there is a parable in this disease and its treatment. People suffering from this disorder suffer from constantly telling themselves a lie that they have a faulty build, which includes flawed or even needless body parts. The whole world might try to convince them otherwise, but the lie has beset their body and mind alike. The treatment for it is in releasing the mind from the insanity of its own false convictions. The sacred story of Creation says that the human being is created in the image of God. That being is capable of communion with God. That God would like His children's body and its members to be kept in the state of a living sacrifice to Him. The resulting intimacy with the Creator alone can undo the blinding lie from the Spirit of falsehood, who is also the Father of lies.

Attempts to shape or reshape ourselves according to our own delusions result only in deconstruction. A depraved mind obeys anything it is told, and may even offer its body for slaughter, all fees paid voluntarily.

Story #99
Smelling Well or Ill

Humans and canines get along well. The canine family has earned uncontested peerage in human service long ago, from the igloo hamlet to the stately home. Mansions or mud huts, the dog is happy with its space, and serves loyally, in all posts of power or play. Lawmen and sportsmen have him on their teams, hunters and fighters harness his strengths. He runs the master's errands in war or peace, facile with force or love. The lurking terrorist dreads the sound of his sniff as much as the blind trust his guiding eye. In a merry home he whips about in shared joy. When the house is left to him alone, he guards it fiercely. All these are true, but is there anything new? Perhaps. How about disease care?

Japanese researchers have trained a Labrador retriever to sniff out cancer in humans. Forget the expensive lab work. Just let him have the breath and stool samples of the patient. Of the 300 specimen sets the dog tested, forty had cancer. Accuracy rates registered at 98%. "Smell diagnosis" has existed for centuries, says Dr. Gary Beauchamp of the Monell Chemical Senses Center in Philadelphia. Every disease has its own peculiar "smell," which turns stronger as the disease worsens, he adds. Beauchamp also related the 2007 news story of a woman who had her dog all of a sudden sniffing at one of her breasts without quitting. Taking that sniff as nothing to sneeze at, she went to the doctor, and sure enough, she had cancer in that breast.

It's not cancer patients alone who would thank the dog for its peril alerts. When sugar levels drop in diabetics, MedicAlert dogs sense it right away. They endearingly force the dependent human to rest and to correct the condition. Again, the dog does this by the sense of smell, which, depending on the breed, is estimated to be a million times stronger than the same power in humans.

The gifts of life and the means of running it appear shed abroad the whole earth and well beyond it. To see that part of our care in the charge of a dog, a hamster, a bird, or a bee makes our shared living space welcomingly intimate. Evidently, the chords of life are pulsed by love as they run through the members of creation in their roles of serving each other.

Story #100
Floating Iron

Elisha is a big name in the history of Israel. He had a public career as the nation's prophet for six decades. Royalty and dignitaries, both domestic and foreign, came under his influence and coveted his counsel and help. Like his master Elijah of equal fame, he had the extraordinary gift of working wonders, which he used solely for the purposes of delivering people from difficulty, rather than for gaining attention or earning praise. Both the master and the disciple lived in 9th century BC.

The master had run a school which trained young men to become prophets. The students were called "sons of the prophets," in the sense that a disciple or an apprentice was treated like a son to the teacher, and the teacher in turn would be a parent to the student.

When Elijah's time on earth was done, instead of normal physical death, he was caught up to heaven in what appeared to be a chariot of fire, driven by horsemen of fire. At that moment Elisha, his prime disciple who literally shadowed the master, cried out: "My father, my father, the chariots and horsemen of Israel!" That was one spontaneous, descriptive line on who Elijah was to the nation. When that chariot appeared, Elisha was physically present as an eyewitness. More importantly, the mantle of Elijah fell from above for Elisha to pick up, which he did. With the mantle on him as the symbol of succession, Elisha carried on serving Israel, though twice as powerfully as had his master, having received a "double portion" of God's grace and power. Now you know where those great English idioms came from — "someone's mantle falling on a person," "double portion," and even "chariots of fire." They are all yours now, no charge.

With the departure of his master, Elisha became the new president of the school. The school was flourishing. They needed more space. The first major campus project of Elisha's tenure seems to have been a building program. One of the student leaders sought Elisha's permission to bring some timber from the jungle of Jordan for the purpose. The prophet agreed. Then they asked for another favor. They didn't want to go by themselves but wanted the prophet to go with them. The prophet agreed, and on they went to the forest.

The young men began their work in earnest. They were felling construction quality timber. Each man was at his tree. All of a sudden they heard someone exclaim that his axehead had flown off the handle. And where did it go? Right into the depth of the river Jordan. None of them seemed to have had any skill in swimming or diving. Perhaps they all were hillbillies. The man who lost the tool began to worry, not just because he lost the axehead, but because the axe was not his own, but had been borrowed. (Read the full record in Chapter 6 of the Second Book of Kings– that's in the Jewish Bible, or what Christians call The Old Testament).

You might think nothing of it to replace an axe today. All it takes is a quick dash to Home Depot, and in the blink of an eye you have a new one, or even a better one, and off you go. Not so in ancient times when iron was scarce and expensive, and travel to an ironworker took far greater investment of time and effort – and even after that, there was no guarantee that an axe-head of equivalent size and quality would be immediately available.

The man's worry concerned the prophet. He is always the resource man, whether for the king, or for the general, or for the peasant. And, in this case, the man who is suffering the anxiety is also "a son of the prophet," remember?

"So, where did your axe fall?", asks the prophet.

The man points to the spot over the river.

Elisha cuts a little stick from a tree branch and throws it over the place. The young men have their eyes set on the floating stick, which seemed to hold its place over the water. In seconds, they notice a small upward thrust of water, as though from some movement underneath. Next thing you know, there is the lost axehead, within arm's reach from the river's edge. "Take it up," says the master. The man reaches out and grabs it.

It is not difficult to see that the young men and their master are of the same faith, but at two levels. Nothing wrong with that. While the young men had permission to go on their timber hunt, they also had the foresight to take the stronger man with them. A prophet worth his salt does not move about without a purpose. He or she goes forth only for the right reason, either already known, or to know at the right time as the full purpose is revealed.

Every spiritual act challenges the natural, because faith is supernatural.

Why is authentic faith neither nervous nor fearful about challenges? Because faith can overpower all challenges.

Every prayer is an act of making iron float.

If you can learn to be on the side of the Spirit of God, what sunk iron might you not be called to raise?

Story #101
A Pair of Legs

The poet John Donne lived dangerously at least for the first half of his life and was slowed down only by extreme outcomes. He studied at Oxford, Cambridge, and Lincoln's Inn, and did well at all of them, yet his Catholic identity deprived him of a college degree. While yet a child, he lost his father who had left him a millionaire's estate by modern terms but, as soon as the son laid hands on it, he blew it all, and lived impoverished for years afterwards. He sailed to the Spanish world as a pirate and returned with nothing. He secured a starter job as the secretary to a state official with whose niece Anne he eloped, only to be caught and thrown into prison, and for the couple to live at the mercy of others for years afterwards.

Things did change, however. A royal favorite commended Donne to King James as someone worthy of patronage. The King was fully aware of his great merits and firmly stated that divinity was Donne's best fit. Let us not forget that, before this, the man was reputed in London as "Jack Donne the Rake." King James must have seen in

Donne something that the rest of the world did not. Donne indeed became a great Anglican divine, filling England's most visible pulpits as the Royal Chaplain and the Dean of St. Paul's Cathedral.

As a public figure, Donne was once asked to join a diplomatic mission to France and to Germany while his pregnant wife was within days of delivery. All care was promised for her, but understandably, the timing troubled him and Anne alike. To comfort the tearful Anne, Donne wrote "A Valediction: Forbidding Mourning," a farewell speech in verse, in which he entreated her not to make the grief between them obvious to others. After all, "our two souls are one," unaffected by separation, he reasoned. However, he went on,

> If they be two, they are two so
> As stiff twin compasses are two:
> Thy soul, the fixed foot, makes no show
> To move, but doth, if the other do;
> . . . .
> Such wilt thou be to me, who must
> Like the other foot obliquely run;
> Thy firmness makes my circle just
> And make me end where I begun.

Donne did leave, as planned. Left alone in dire sorrow, ten days later, Anne delivered a baby in stillbirth. Her husband, alone in his room in France, had a vision of the grievous scene. Nonetheless, we may rightly thank Anne who inspired her husband's unforgettable imagery of the compass.

He saw himself as the roaming leg of the compass, which needed the steady strength from the firm leg that Anne was – and that firm leg was what made his motion possible.

But perhaps there is more to what he said to Anne. Is their story not the figurative journey of Everyman? Do we not run the race of life on paired legs, one visible and the other invisible? Does every expression of life not have an invisible enablement along with it? We run no more on our own than does the compass leg, which can move only if the other stays firm in the center. A Quiet Power runs obliquely with our feeble limbs, until life's course is run and done. Somehow, we are important enough in the eye of heaven for such remarkable care.

The End

Index of Titles

Study or Discussion Questions

1. Many stories in this collection narrate teaching and learning experiences. Have you found any striking tips that you could apply in your own teaching or learning?

2. Samuel Scudder recalls the taskmaster style of Louis Agassiz's personal mode of pedagogy. Between their first meeting and Scudder's later recollection of it, what must have changed the thinking and learning style of Scudder?

3. In "Fenelon as Teacher," what principles did the great man inculcate in his royal pupil? And how did he do so?

4. "Poverty in Mansions" may be seen as a case of blindness in "furnishing." Is there a correspondence between the furnishing of one's dwelling and the furnishing of one's mind?

5. Adversity, affliction, or poverty tend to impact one's formation beneficently. In hindsight, affliction proves to be a strong contributor to greatness. Examine how this

truth shows in "Don't Worry, Mama Will Be Praying," "Ekalavya and Drona," "Philoctetes' Wound," "The Pearl of Great Price" or "The Pain of the Painless."

6. Figurative or poetic elements of language deepen communication. Stories such as "A Pair of Legs," "The Screaming Sign," "Two Windows," "A Wrestler's Lines," "The Weaver's Shuttle," or "The Rod of Levi" go beyond the plain sense of the surface. Make your own observations of how the metaphors and symbols in them become vehicles of ideas.

7. "Bridge Yourself," "Tell Me Who I am," "Messiah among the Monks" "The Unspared Strength," among others, show the need for us to connect with others for meaningful existence. Discuss these stories as parables of community life and thoughtful citizenship.

8. Philosophers like St Augustine, Blaise Pascal, and John Calvin discuss depravity as an inherent condition of humans. They believe that true knowledge should have redemptive virtue which would raise humans from the animal world to the angelic. How does that apply in "The Bullet Fee," "The Dare Death Diner," "The Cannibal Call," "Loot on Display," "The Unblessable," "A Law to Flee," and "Child Mothers"?

9. What might stories such as "The Animals of Job," "The Spider's Chide," and "The Trickle's Push" say about unrecognized, unused or at least underused potential in people?

10. What do stories such as "The Waterman" and "Shoot before the Strike" say about gifts and talents?

11. Can you share a memorable personal experience or a surprise discovery of yours with an audience? Good autobiographies contain numerous personal stories of their narrators. Read some of them and see how you can connect with an audience likewise. Suggested examples (though not included in this book) would be the learning stories of Benjamin Franklin, Amanda Berry Smith, and Booker T. Washington, for a start.

12. Every story has a spiritual reality or a dimension to it. The experience narrated in it corresponds to a spiritual principle accepted or resisted. Examine any story in this book from the viewpoint of this claim.

13. The purpose of a fable, parable, or an exemplum is to teach and learn by its evident similarity to another object of reference. List the ways in which you can use stories in presentations.

14. Conventional teaching moves from theory to example. Parabolic teaching puts the illustration first and provides the theory afterwards. If you have not tried that paradigm, try to see which of the stories in this book might fit discussion opportunities of your discipline, a class you must teach, or a talk, and reflect on how that shapes your message.

15. The stories you have read here have global contexts. Are there some that gave you an "epiphanic" moment, a culture shock, or advantages of comparative understanding? With our assumptions of political correctness and personal space in the Western world, how might you respond to the moral authority that the Desert Fathers or Mr. Udappachar exercised?

About

Pippa Rann
Books & Media

Pippa Rann Books & Media and Global Resilience Publishing are imprints of Salt Desert Media Group Ltd., U.K., distributed by Gardners in the UK, and in 17 Asian countries by Penguin Random House India.

Salt Desert Media Group Ltd. is a British company that was founded in 2019, and is a Member of the Independent Publishers Guild. At present, the company has two imprints, Pippa Rann Books & Media and Global Resilience Publishing.

Global Resilience Publishing (GRP), as the name suggests, has a truly international remit. A non-fiction imprint, GRP focuses on global challenges and opportunities, and on how we can address those as a global community. Such challenges include Climate Change, the Global Financial System, Multilateral Governance (e.g., the

United Nations), Public-Private Partnership, Leadership, System Change, Corporate Governance, Family Firms, Global Values, Global Philanthropy, Commercial Sponsorship, and New Technologies including Artificial Intelligence. Two things make GRP unique as an imprint; first, our books take a global perspective (not the perspective of a particular nation); second, GRP focuses exclusively on such global challenges. GRP is scheduled to begin operations in Autumn 2021, and the first publications are planned for release in 2022.

By contrast, Pippa Rann Books & Media, launched on August the 17th, 2020, focuses wholly on India and on the Indian diaspora. The first title was published in Autumn 2020 - is Avay Shukla's PolyTicks, DeMocKrazy & MumboJumbo: Babus, Mantris and Netas (Un)Making Our Nation. Since then, we have published Sudhakar Menon's Seeking God, Seeking Moksha, Jyoti Guptara's Business Storytelling From Hype to Hack, Sudeep Sen's collection of poems and photographs, Anthropocene: Climate Change, Contagion, Consolation, and Mantras for Positive Ageing, edited by Padma Shri Dr V. Mohini Giri and Meera Khanna, with a Foreword by H. H. The Dalai Lama.

However, our entire publishing schedule has been upset by the pandemic, as have the entire lives of millions of people. If there is no other significant disruption, we are planning to release in 2021, in addition to The Village Maestro and 100 Other Stories, the following books:

- Brijraj Singh's *In Arden: A Memoir of Four Years in Shillong, 1974 to 1978*

- Dr Valson Thampu's *Beyond Religion: Imaging A New Humanity*

- Catherine Ann Jones's *East or West?: Stories of India* (especially commissioned for the 75th anniversary of India's independence)

and

- Dr. Anthony P. Stone's *Hindu Astrology: Myths, Symbols and Realities.*

Books planned for 2022 include *Distant Goddess* (the English translation of a memoir by the outstanding British graphic artist and illustrator, Biman Mullick), and an anthology of Indian poetry in English, specially compiled for the 75th anniversary of Indian independence.

Books that are at various stages of commissioning and production include *Indian Actors on the British*

Screen, Indian Cricketers in British Cricket, After Hindutva What? The History & Prospects of Liberalism in India, and *Bollywood Spirituality.*

We are always open to first class ideas for books, provided complete manuscripts can be turned in on time. Please note that Pippa Rann Books & Media focuses entirely and exclusively on publishing material that nurtures, among Indians as well as among others who love India, the values of democracy, justice, liberty, equality, and fraternity.

That means we publish:

(a) Books and media by authors of Indian origin, on any subject that broadly serves the purpose mentioned above

and

(b) Books and media by authors of non-Indian origin, on any subject connected with India or with the Indian diaspora, which serves the purpose mentioned above - again, broadly interpreted.

Global Resilience Publishing and Pippa Rann Books & Media are only two of several imprints that are conceived of, and will be launched, God willing, by Salt Desert Media Group Ltd., U. K. The imprints will cover different regions of the globe, different themes, and so on. And if you have an idea for a new imprint that you would like to establish, please get in touch.

Prabhu Guptara, the Publisher of Salt Desert Media Group, says, "For all our imprints, and for the attainment of our incredibly high vision, we need your support. Whatever your gifts and abilities, you are welcome to support us with the most precious gift of your time. The *seva* you do is not for us but is for the sake of our nation, and for the world as a whole. Please email us with your email, location, and phone contact details on **publisher@pipparannbooks.** com, letting us know what you feel you can do. Could you be an organiser or greeter at our events? Could you ring people on our behalf? Write to people? Write guest blogs or articles? Write a regular column? Do interviews? Help with electronic media, social media, or general marketing? Connect us with people you know who might be willing to help in some way or other?"

He adds, "I am one man working from his dining table, so I do not and cannot keep up with everything that is happening in India, let alone in the world. There are many challenges and numerous opportunities - help me to understand what these are. Pass information on to me that could be useful to me. Put your ideas to me. Any and all insights from you are most welcome, as they will multiply our joint effectiveness. It is only as we work together that we can contribute effectively to changing our nation and our world for the better".

Join our mailing list to discover Pippa Rann Books which will inform you on a wide range of topics, and inspire as well as equip you as an individual, as a member of your family, and as someone who loves India.

www.pipparannbooks.com